The Colonisation of Mars

The Story of One Family: The Fishers

Donald E. White

A.H. STOCKWELL
PUBLISHERS SINCE 1898

The Colonisation of Mars
Published in 2024 by
Donald E. White
in association with
Arthur H Stockwell Ltd
ahstockwell.co.uk

To my children and grandchildren. Seize the day!

Contents

Note to Readers

I am William Henry, a member of the second generation of humans born on Mars and a Fisher by birthright.

I am now 56 years of age and have time on my hands, so I decided to record my version of life in the Fisher families who were important in the colonisation of Mars.

I record this so that my children and future generations may know something about their ancestors before my memories fade.

I do not claim historical accuracy, for my memories are undoubtedly biased and partial.

Those seeking true histories should visit the archives of Mars, which contain all this information gathered by COMAS 1, our original and dedicated computer.

William

THE FIRST FAMILY
Mars Wave Colony

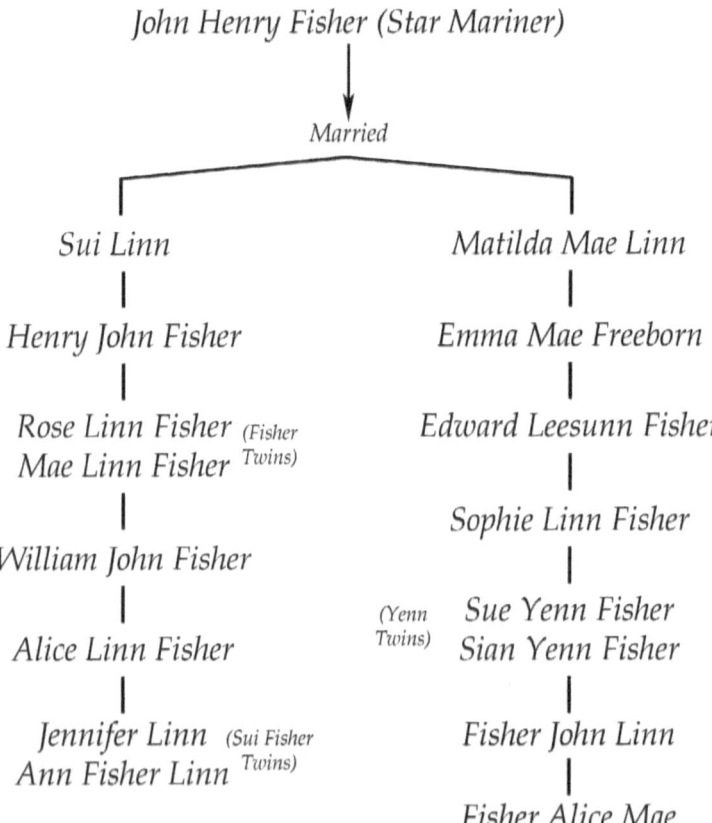

John Henry Fisher (Star Mariner)

Married

Sui Linn

Henry John Fisher

Rose Linn Fisher *(Fisher*
Mae Linn Fisher *Twins)*

William John Fisher

Alice Linn Fisher

Jennifer Linn *(Sui Fisher*
Ann Fisher Linn *Twins)*

Matilda Mae Linn

Emma Mae Freeborn

Edward Leesunn Fisher

Sophie Linn Fisher

(Yenn Sue Yenn Fisher
Twins) Sian Yenn Fisher

Fisher John Linn

Fisher Alice Mae

Mars: An Introduction

Mankind had been an observer of the night sky from the first days of taking shelter from predators and achieving some sort of security. Often hungry and cold, but at least for a time with a chance of rest, most gathered to a fire or huddled in a group to stay warm and comfortable. Others, perhaps on guard duty or perhaps hardier, watched as the night sky wheeled above their heads and wondered what the future might hold. The stars, those lights in the sky, were obviously signs from the gods, higher beings and the arbiters of the fate of every man or woman.

As time and generations passed, gifted observers discerned patterns and began to attribute meaning to the procession of these 'lights' across the heavens, developing associations with actions relevant to their small but important lives. Some believed they could divine the patterns related to good and evil, fortune and failure, success and disaster.

These interpreters became important; as men became more powerful, they increasingly turned to the Oracles and to wizards for guidance.

The planets, our companions in our little solar system, were given importance in these divinations, and so Saturn became a symbol for power; Jupiter for wisdom; Mars, a red star, the colour of blood, for war; Venus, veiled in beauty, for love and Mercury, the little fast-moving one, for speed and communication.

With the development of telescopes and far-seeing technologies, observation became something practised as a specialisation in the field of science. Mankind began to dream of voyages to such distant worlds. The moon, our close companion, was the first target and was achieved at great cost in the twentieth century.

The next great venture must surely be the planet Mars, a harsh environment – now a frozen world despite the red colour of its terrain. The best twenty-first century technology could do was to investigate it robotically and so the race for the establishment of a human colony was further delayed. But our astral dreams only gathered greater momentum.

This story is about that imagined destiny and its fulfilment.

Chapter One

Throughout the twentieth century, mankind strove to cope with conflict and disruption to the life of the ever-increasing population. The destruction of cities and devastation of great areas of land grew as weapons became ever more potent.

By the twenty-first century, the accumulated waste from the demands of so many people built to alarming levels and became a major factor in man's impact on the climate of Earth. Methane and carbon dioxide in the atmosphere was causing rising temperatures, loss of ice at the poles and rising sea levels. Viable living space was being destroyed.

The populations of Earth – controlled by organisations called states – competed for use of the finite resources of the planet, which were at that time used to move folk, feed them, and produce that benefit they called profit. Most in these early days used carbon-based fuels like oil, gas and some solar sources to produce the energy they needed.

Scientists became increasingly aware of the damage being caused to the climate itself by all this primitive use of resources. As the new generations of people became more highly educated, awareness of the problems became more widespread, and the ordinary people themselves began to call for change.

By 2020 the damage caused by global warming was becoming a cause célèbre with more and more young people demanding action to ensure that they and their children had a future on Earth. Gradually those in power recognised that a serious effort must be made to halt the temperature rises and very specific support introduced to achieve a guarantee of continued life. Despite adapting technology and inventing new mechanical aids to support us in alien environments, the need for a fundamental change on Earth was upon us.

In terms of energy, wind power was proving useful and atomic power generation was working but was increasingly expensive to produce and the disposal of waste with a half-life of thousands of years was a real problem.

Power was mainly provided by burning fossil fuels such as coal, gas and wood, all of which caused further discharge of carbon dioxide into the atmosphere.

New methods of power generation were becoming essential. Newly developed battery technology led to a massive switch, driving the 2030s to solar-powered battery-stored energy sources. Since the 2020s, scientists had used electric vehicles and private and public transport systems on Earth to provide cleaner forms of mobility. Attention also turned to hydrogen-burning engines, to small fusion engines, although these were not economic.

By the 2050s these efforts, plus a re-wildlife and re-forestation programme, were beginning to ameliorate the changes to the climate of Earth. There was also a switch to vegetarianism and a reduction in the use of land for farming as more efficient greenhouse towers were built and used to grow crops for human consumption.

The scientific exploration of space within the cosmos had been going on for generations, built on the work and collaboration between NASA and the Russian space industry. This co-operation had produced off-Earth workshops and space stations for exploration vehicles reaching out through our solar system and beyond.

With living conditions off Earth becoming more accessible, the rich and wealthy demanded a place or places be set aside for their private use and pleasure. Eventually some satellite rings were built for this purpose: the first, over New York, was called Elysium after the paradise of Greek mythology.

The rich folk, of course, needed servants of all kinds, technicians, engineers and scientists to maintain these cities and parks in the sky, so the populations of the satellites grew ever larger and became cities in their own right.

By the end of the twenty-first century the engineers and scientists made a breakthrough in the use of electromagnetic engines. The electromagnetic elevation units, which had been used for generations to power swift-moving trains, were allied to linear magnetic power, resulting in a technology capable of projecting a vehicle at very high speeds because of the lack of friction and drag.

This programme brought immediate rewards: Earth's transport systems were adapted and all ships, planes and transport vehicles were converted to this maglev system.

The next logical step was for such maglev systems to run all transport to the satellite cities, the space workshops and off-Earth stations.

Naturally science teams now turned their investigations of our solar systems towards the prospect of colonisation.

Colonisation was going to be costly, so the wealthy satellite cities were asked to provide finance to support the development of large transport vehicles called Arks, capable of carrying, say, one hundred thousand people. Any city offering to help would be given the chance to nominate citizens to be sent to Mars. Of course these citizens – and they should be young – must have completed their education, preferably at a university and be willing participants.

Quite a few city satellites refused to co-operate but eventually provided finance and a team of volunteers, so by the year 2101 the programme was inaugurated with a great fanfare and celebration by Earth media. It was decided that each Ark would carry two females for every male.

The women would create a strong matriarchy and would eventually lead the new Martian Colony. This decision was much disputed at first, for it was clearly intended to overcome the potential for male domination and antagonistic behaviour. However female participation in Earth affairs was already strong and the decision of the Colony organiser was finally accepted.

The project became a reality when all the future colonists gathered at Cape Canaveral for training and the inauguration of the three-year education programme. It was acknowledged immediately that some of these young people might fail and some reserve candidates were pre-selected as possible substitutes.

Four years later, the New Wave colonists were ready to go. My story concerns some of them. The Earth/Mars transit system that had been carrying out scientific research and mapping had always been run from Earth by computer systems; artificial intelligence had been used to 'man' the transit vehicles, though some of these were human duplicates (replicants).

Of course control was only possible if earthside computer-based technology continued to function without hitch or interruption. Consequently robots had been constructed to 'work' the vehicles and were slaved to an on-board AI controller. A small crew of humans – thee or four – would accompany each vehicle, all accredited members of the Starlight Navigation Institute, to offer manual control in the event of catastrophic failure.

The Replicants were designed to look like perfect specimens of the various races but some were fashioned as irregular. Human reactions to such creatures, if we can call them that, was interesting but not always positive.

Each Ark and its colonists would have access to such comforts.

Chapter Two

Launch

The launch day finally loomed and all the First Wave voyagers began to congregate at the conference centre in Starlight Navigation Headquarters at Cape Canaveral. They greeted each other with some caution but quite quickly it became clear that they were adaptable, quite friendly and healthy.

The media worldwide were eager to interview each and every one, especially those individuals from their own cities. Face-to-face discussions were conducted and recorded for posterity. Some participants were a bit reticent but those willing to co-operate found great favour and support. At home parents, siblings and other relatives enjoyed their moment of fame too.

Scientific advisors and historians, even amateur ones, were consulted and asked to forecast future success and to hint at a possible leader of the new Colony. All this material would be retained for research and reuse at some future time. Mankind as a nomad roving the cosmos was a popular idea.

Not every city and country was involved and it became increasingly clear that those who had failed to join were considered second class. The response was predictable: China, India and Latin America announced the establishment of programmes of colonisation of their own. China was particularly upset; they had been visiting Mars for over sixty years and already had an established research programme run by robot and AI systems, although sited far from the site chosen as a base for the Eurocentric Colony.

Chapter Three

Departure day finally arrived and every media channel carried pictures of lift-off and all the attendant ceremonies. Most of the speeches were boring and predictable but each was recorded, future use in mind.

Lift-off was an anti-climax; each craft lifted gently and without fuss and fire into the stratosphere, only then to accelerate at speed as the gravitational pull of Earth receded.

The Arks travelled together as a group with the minimum of disturbance, all under the central control of the master computer programme COMAS, which was directly linked to each Ark command centre.

The journey would take nearly six months to complete and communication links with Earth and its satellite cities would be maintained once a day throughout this period.

Navigation Institute leaders would hold each briefing and respond to questions from Earth. A separate period of time was set aside for individual members of the First Wave to communicate with family, friends and their home cities if they so desired. Many travellers worked this communication link with enthusiasm, at least at first, but gradually life on board the Ark began to dominate. On Earth, life for most resumed normality.

Chapter Four

Travelling On

As the voyage progressed quite a few of the travellers began to find that time was dragging. They had little to do, not even cooking and cleaning, for all this was done by robots. Only the ones with actual work, such as nursing and medical staff used to give a human touch to those needing care, felt useful. Consequently indolence led to worries and in some cases even to depression.

COMAS and its servers were charged with the duty of overall care for the Colonists and quietly they were beginning to amass information about each individual, looking for signs of weakness – either physical or mental – and also seeking potential for leadership. Even the most intelligent had problems to offset and skills that were limited, perhaps to the theoretical.

Entertainment by TV games and computer programmes was eventually deemed insufficient. COMAS decided these people needed to inaugurate a weekly dance – in other words, something of an event, something to look forward to and to plan and prepare for. These might also lead to wider liaison between representatives of the various cities, and perhaps also encourage diversification in the choice of partners. The more cosmopolitan society could become would also widen the potential gene pool.

The first problem to overcome was that music tastes varied so amongst humans, so a series of experimental broadcasts paraded various styles and monitored take-up. An unexpected bonus was the creation of bands and groups from among the travellers themselves; many seemingly had musical talent. Each of the male and female groups began to gather followers and quite quickly others participated too. All good so far.

The dance and music programme was a success and a number of weddings and partnerships were formed as involvement grew.

Next to receive attention was clothing and dress. This led to the establishment of weekend get-togethers between individuals with design flair, who perhaps might continue to work together.

Lastly, the computers suggested the establishment of regular athletic meetings. Gymnasium and training equipment was unpacked and installed in dedicated space. Some took advantage immediately and it was only a few weeks later that inter-group competitions were set up: idleness was becoming rare.

The organised monthly dances proved extremely popular. Music was mostly played by live bands with intervals during which canned recordings of Earth-side musicians would be broadcast.

Food and drink were available but excessive consumption was discouraged. The dancers were free to display their particular talents and many dance forms would be catered for during the course of the evening. Some drew strong support and were well attended. Waltzes, line dancing, Latino forms and – rather surprisingly – courtly and country dances.

Everyone therefore had a chance to shine and perhaps attract the attention of a lover or potential partner.

Sometimes – and inevitably – trouble would develop, because humans are so competitive, but anger would be frowned upon and aggression punished. Everyone knew they were being watched and even recorded and that the robot guards were authorised to use limited force to restore calm. In extreme situations they were permitted to end a fight or physical attack by the use of low-power tazers that would render the aggressor unconscious.

A tazer incident would be recorded on the individual's profile and records. It was a case of literally 'three strikes and you are out' for an undesirable male or female. This action would be automatic, but one appeal to a Courts Martial would be permitted.

The dancers generally approved; these dances were occasions for enjoyment, laughter and love – not for fighting.

Chapter Five

The mood and the wellbeing of the whole wave of the settlers was now improving rapidly. Couples were now meeting, weddings and partnerships booming. Many young women were now pregnant and looking forward to motherhood. The first Women's Institute meeting would take place in one month's time.

With the rise in pregnancy there was an increasing need for a pre-natal service and the medical staff began to get really busy. Robots could assess condition but most women preferred human females to assist and provide personal care.

By the end of month four, nearly two thousand women and girls were pregnant and the pressure on the medical services was very high. Our Clan Mother Sui Linn was one of the staff affected; she, a student intern serving in the maternity unit, was working full shifts daily.

It can be no surprise that as a consequence she was tired and a bit tense at the end of each day. She could not relax enough to go to her rest, so she started to seek solitude and time to think. The place she chose to visit was the Planetarium and Observation Deck, thinking about the day's events and problems whilst viewing the stars in all their serene beauty. She needed peace and in this place, – generally alone because of the hour – she found it.

The Observation Deck was quite popular but only with a small number of travellers. Most preferred to be where many congregated, where they could meet with friends and often where the music and conversation was loud and engaging.

Amongst the smaller group were many who were interested in the changing view of our solar system, already thinking about the night skies on Mars and facing this future with some reservations.

The planetarium was less used at this time mainly because the skies most often showed the views from Earth. Just occasionally a programme showing the Martian skies would be screened and this attracted much more interest and so many questions that eventually that programme became standard and the Earth scenes returned to store, ready for use in future curricula.

Occasionally a lecturer would attend in order to answer questions and explain some of the scenes shown, often of violent winds and dust storms.

The lecturer was always a serving officer with the Navigation Institute acting as an observer 'On Deck' as they called the control room.

One of the most interesting of the speakers was a youngish officer on his maiden voyage. He was called John Henry Fisher; at one time in his youth he had served in the British Navy. His observations were often acute and he seemed absorbed in every aspect of star and planetary life before him.

Very late one evening, Sui Linn visited the Observation Lounge and was quietly watching the night sky. John Henry had just finished a tour of duty and came into the chamber to think. He failed to notice Sui Linn sunk in a couch nearby and as usual did not call for light. Sui knew he was there but did not draw attention to herself. She could not resist the temptation to watch him unobserved.

John settled himself, then took out his iPad and started to write, occasionally stopping to watch some movement around the Milky Way. She was intrigued and curious but left him alone. She must have dozed off at some point; she was really comfortable. John was speaking into his com unit and Sui realised she could hear the responses from COMAS. It all sounded very intimate. John finally left about an hour or so later; Sui stayed and dozed off for a comfortable sleep right where she was.

Next day was very pressurised, as more and more girls were enrolling for testing and to reserve space in the maternity ward.

When she did leave work, she returned with a friend to the nurses' accommodation block.

Sui could not forget her night near John and she returned to the Observation Lounge the next night hoping to see more of him. She did! This time John was already there and was surprised when she approached to talk with him.

They started talking about the scene before them and when he mentioned his interests included Deep Space, they went together to the Planetarium where he called up a special programme about the Crab Nebula in Taurus and the Eagle Nebula in Serpens showing massive dust clouds, where stars were being born and the legendary Black Holes abound.

She asked him if this was what he was talking about with COMAS.

"No," John replied. "That programme was looking at comets and debris activity that might impact on the life of the Mars Colony in the reasonably near future. These objects are mostly particles and gasses left over when our solar system was forming. Some containing ice and iron might also be a source of other minerals and could be useful in the future."

"COMAS reports to you, then?" she asked.

"Well no, but the computer knows I have a particular interest in such research and keeps me informed. COMAS and I have much in common in these investigations."

John called up a different programme dealing with the creation of Black Holes, which occur when a sun implodes.

"There is much speculation about these on Earth," he said, "and more and more are being discovered at this time. We speculate that such holes draw all surrounding matter into the vortex and wonder what happens to all the materials absorbed. Also, some think these holes could link to other alternative universes! Why should our set of universes be the only ones created? What if Big Bangs are still occurring" It's all very interesting to think upon.

"This colonisation attempt is therefore an experiment to see if mankind can establish a viable base, if you like a model which could be improved upon and help colonial peoples in the future.

I am personally sure that the Earth will recover equilibrium if humans give it time, but colonising our solar system could still be a great benefit for future generations, including children, as a result of this initiative.

"Our Mars programme will enable humankind to assess the benefits of such experiments, but there is no doubt our group will face many challenges in the years ahead.

Mars is alien territory – we can land, set up bases using the equipment, science and technology we have now that was designed to assist our rocket-propelled exploration of space – but we may find developing this into habitable lands to meet the demands of our people a daunting task. "Mars is only about one-tenth the size of Earth, it is frozen deeply and very far from our solar system, so warmth and gravitational adjustment will be crucial to success. Many, even amongst our groups, talk of terraforming quite glibly, but such talk is idle. It will take thousands of years to achieve such an environment and the problems we will encounter may prove insuperable.

"Fusion power systems may help but so far such experiments as take place on Earth consume more energy than they generate.

"We speculate about using other forces, perhaps Dark Matter, gravitational pulls to move from and through space. Black holes might be useful someday."

Sui was intrigued.

"I have heard about these speculations," she said, "but can see little point in pursuing such ideas. As I understand it a Black Hole is like a massive whirlpool from which nothing at all can escape. The idea of investigating such a phenomenon seems crazy – if nothing can escape the pull, even light, how could you report your findings?"

"I know," said John, "but scientists will still pursue such impossible dreams – who knows where mankind's interest will take us?"

They spent the next few nights in debate but it was intruding on their sleep and they were getting nowhere as a couple.

Night after night they talked until exhausted, then fell asleep, sometimes where they sat. They often woke up in each other's arms. Comfortable together, they sought to be together more and more – indeed, a day apart seemed wasteful. It was no surprise when during their third week John gave Sui a kiss.

Sui did not respond but she definitely 'felt something', so the next night she took the initiative and they kissed and cuddled instead of talking and discussing. The pattern of their evenings switched to the personal from this point on and fairly soon they were discussing living together permanently. The sex was wonderful.

Despite their passionate need to be together. they were both sufficiently intelligent enough to realise commitment would involve them in a way neither had ever considered before. John, as a Navigation Officer, had planned to spend his life voyaging and had refused serious involvement with several young women over the last year in order to further his career and pursue his ambition to lead exploration of the stars.

Sui, though only eighteen, was pursuing a career path that would lead to qualification as a gene doctor, though her true interest was more in the world of biology, micro biology and genetic science.

Talking things over in the quiet of their apartments, they tried to be rational. What were they doing, drifting into a relationship that one or both would regret? Or were they now prepared to consider the surrender of their ambitions, friends and lifestyles in order to be together? For a few days the tension between them caused much unhappiness, particularly for Sui Linn who still had ties to her family at home in San Francisco and to her sister Matilda Mae – known as Tilda – who was travelling with them. Matilda had suggested this liaison was simply the effect of suddenly discovering a strong sex drive and would pass.

John, quite a solitary man, tried very hard to be rational: he would have to ask formally for permission to marry from his Senior Captain. His employment record would be impaired and he might even be required to leave that employment altogether, never to travel as he had always expected to do. He could understand that, even if he was permitted to serve, a conflict of interest must arise. Voyaging through our solar system takes time and would lead to long periods of being apart, making Sui the modern equivalent of a sea wife of old Earth: short periods of ecstatic togetherness punctuated by long absences. Modern computer-based technology would enable them to communicate but would not permit close liaison.

He decided to ask Sui to agree to a short period of absence, say a month, when they would simply not communicate at all. He would request a temporary transfer to another Ark, after explaining the situation to his Captain. Reluctantly Sui agreed; Tilda thought this wise.

A few days later they said their goodbyes and John departed. Sui, accompanied now by Tilda, breathed a sigh of relief as this pressure lifted.

Unfortunately the relief was short-lived: she was becoming more and more restless as the days of separation passed. What was John doing now? Perhaps some girl on the other Ark had taken his love away? "Don't be silly," said Tilda. "If you cannot stand separation for even a few days, how would you manage to survive a long period of enforced absence? And what would you do about children at such times?"

Sui tried to relax.

John was profoundly unhappy: he had never indulged in sexual pleasures for any length of time and now he missed it. The girl replicants on this new vessel were available for relief but he was mooning about each day and fantasising about Sui most nights. Even his interest in the solar system and the asteroids had waned. What if Sui had given him up? Some other guy might have moved in. No, surely not – he would kill him!

Sensibly he settled down. What the hell was he thinking? Only one week apart and he was desperate to get back to the NY Ark. He took a sedative and at last managed to sleep.

Slowly, very slowly, the month of separation passed. John organised a brief expedition to an asteroid with his commander and tried to concentrate. Even as COMAS landed him on the rock, he found himself searching the stars for a sight of the nine Arks in formation. Heigh ho!

Returning to home – the NY Ark – a couple of days later, he was overjoyed to see Sui and Matilda waiting at the embarkation point. They came together in a rush of emotion: together at last. Tilda

14

slipped away totally unnoticed "So much for rationality then!" she thought.

In a blaze of emotion all was swept aside, so John asked for permission to marry, and after a brief delay this was granted, The Captain would perform the ceremony in one week's time. John and his captain dressed specially for the occasion in full dress uniform, and Sui was a vision in white silk: their union became a source of pleasure for many. They were also allocated senior style married quarters. Of course all his fellow officers were intrigued; most had bed companions, but marriage? A major step and commitment indeed.

The younger Colony people were less enthusiastic and many thought Sui foolish to fall for an older man. John Henry was already 38 years old and star men often died young. John and Sui ignored all such negativity; they were by now deeply in love and committed.

Chapter Six

Freedom is a very wonderful thing, but many took time to adjust: so far their lives had been bound up with the wishes, desires and often the ambitions of others. To be free, uninhibited and able to indulge themselves caused some of these wonderful young people to go off the rails and to explore sensations of all kinds.

COMAS and its servers looked on but made no judgement; excesses were noted but as long as common sense reasserted itself in due course they were not registered permanently. Of course some folk did not re-establish sanity and notes were recorded to ensure these individuals were not offered too many chances to cause mischief. A number ended up on the register of undesirables.

There was a strong move among those experimenting to establish pods or communes that would be mutually supportive; ones where love and cohabiting were increasingly random. Surprisingly, perhaps, some of the children eventually born on Mars to such parents would show sings of high awareness. Could a foetus learn?

Matilda moved out of the apartment she had shared with Sui in order to make accommodation available for one of the communes to expand its base. She was asked to join them but decided she much preferred to be independent and free from ties. Actually, she was spending increasing periods of time at the maternity clinic anyway, for Sui was already pregnant and was often nauseous. Just ten weeks after the wedding and the attendant celebrations, Sui for the first time had failed to bleed; she had waited until it was time for the second period before taking a pregnancy test, but this only confirmed what she already knew: she was now carrying a child.

John was now overjoyed: he had waited many years before finding a girl he could respect and love and the prospect of creating a new family with Sui was both exciting and personally fulfilling. He thanked God above and the starlight that had led him to this moment.

They both considered themselves secular people but that night they prayed, while listening to music together and then celebrated with a truly passionate session. Even the next day John found it difficult to leave Sui and return to the Bridge. Sui signed on at the maternity unit, joining all the other potential mothers, not only a member of staff but at last a full participant herself.

Weeks then months of bucolic bliss passed as they discussed future plans, and got to know each other – their pleasures and dislikes.

Chapter Seven

The liaison with John brought many benefits to Sui: gone was the desire to be in with the 'top crowd, the party-goers, movers and shakers, many of whom had great ambitions to fulfil and the drive and energy to push connections and ideas to the limit. She had moved on to a different – not necessarily better – phase but found herself somewhat marginalised. Living in married quarters definitely did not help but it did tweak her group of friends in surprising ways. She asked for a piano and started to learn to play.

Sui was studying hard for her Doctorate but her interest in conception and changes wrought in the bodies and physical appearance of her friends led to a heightened interest in genetics. She talked about these things with John, of course, but – typically male – he was more interested in the science rather than the physical.

Sui was fortunate to have Tilda voyaging with her and although her interests were agriculture and plant genetics, she found her very willing to talk to discuss and evaluate Sui's ideas. Tilda played the piano too! So they duetted. Weeks later, Sui and Tilda began to think about this rather special group they were adventuring with, and when Tilda suggested they try to construct a record of their colleagues and themselves, they found some work in this field had already been undertaken by earthside universities and the record donated to COMAS.

John suggested they ask COMAS to present a programme on the daily closed TV network on this subject, and see if their colleagues were interested and prepared to co-operate in collating a genetics and clinical record.

The programme was approved six weeks later. It was received well but with some adverse reaction too; many felt this information was private and of concern only to themselves. But gradually more and more women came to Sui and Tilda to discuss what would be involved. Momentum was building.

The group organising the Future Matriarchal Council became interested too and some weeks later extended an invitation to Sui and Tilda asking them to explain the reasons this research was necessary, what they hoped to achieve and what the supposed benefit to their little Colony might be. The girls gathered their material, marshalled their ideas and attended. After due consideration and some detailed probing questions, the Council – mostly already pregnant – agreed to support the research and the questioning of individuals. Full original data was already available, based on genetic makeup and DNA. Now individuals would be asked to contribute family histories, details of race and handed-down stories to fill out the record for future generations.

The interview process would be private but recorded by COMAS and her servers: it would only enter the official records after review and sanction by the candidates. Sui and Tilda now had more than enough work on their timetables and so they were given permission to employ three assistant researchers, if willing girls could be found. They were and the project got underway quickly.

Co-operation was of course voluntary and some chose not to co-operate; others were found who had little or no knowledge of their families. The majority, though, approved and co-operated fully. A new society in the making: what could be more important! To acknowledge one's ancestors was a great idea. The fund of tales grew but some consideration had to be given to the possibility of exaggeration, so those stories that were difficult to verify were only included as hearsay, and annotated as such.

A fascinating cross-section of human history was being uncovered.

One evening towards the end of the fifth month of her pregnancy, Sui was sitting watching the news broadcast and cuddling her belly, alone in the early evening – as usual, she thought. John was in his study, reading and talking with COMAS and she felt really piqued.

He had not changed at all, while she was not only carrying a growing child but had witnessed the progressive deterioration of her body shape and energy. It was not fair and she cursed all men. Her mood became increasingly tender and self-pitying.

She felt like storming along to his study and demanding his attention. However she realised that she was being irrational at the moment. John loved, even doted on, her and would respond immediately, but he would not really understand her emotional turmoil: she needed support.

Quietly she left a message on the screen telling John she had gone to join her friends and Tilda, then stumbled along the corridor to the maternity units. In the rest room adjoining the treatment rooms she found six or eight girls she knew and worked with. Some were quiet but more were talking, wailing and complaining one to another: of course, all were pregnant just like Sui. She joined the circle and made her own contribution, feeling immediate relief at finding such a supportive audience.

One of the trained midwives joined them and with calm supportive love eased them all. Thank God for friends, she thought.

Chapter Eight

All this turmoil in the lives of the female voyagers had not gone unnoticed. More and more of the young men were now being left to their own devices and pleasure, and felt somewhat redundant. The sex replicants were a great comfort and solace but increasingly the young men began to frequent the bars to drink, play and encourage or challenge each other, often leaving a bar only in the small hours, drunk and sometimes belligerent too.

Another great recreation was to exchange stories of their individual potency in bed; their conquests and their stamina in performance. Naturally the less successful either kept quiet or boasted of their capabilities, often exaggerating.

In these sessions many referred to girls who were expecting a child as 'pregnant pussy'. The girls got to hear these derogatory comments and were incensed. They got together to talk with their leaders and decided to change the name of the Women's Institute to The Madonna Association. They also let it be known that in future they would expect to be spoken to in terms of respect. 'Donna' was acceptable, 'Pussies' they were not: moreover, the 'Wildcats' would soon unleash their feline instincts and punish the lads if they continued to insult them. The term Pregnant Pussies was soon dropped.

The women in this way showed they would act together and change things if they so desired: a valuable lesson to them all.

Everyone was learning. Most of these young people had come from university where they had just begun to learn the benefits of collaboration. If they intended to found a colony in an alien place, then working with and for each other would become a fact of life.

Naturally, not every Voyager made the change easily but COMAS observation showed those who were failing to adjust and might face problems in the future. Isolation would be considered very seriously. One coupled pair were in rather a distressed state and observation showed that violence and intimidation was occurring. The couple were arrested and the man, Edwin Arlott, was incarcerated for three weeks under supervision.

The young woman, Sally Linn, was upset and at times quite unreasonable in her demands to be re-united with Edwin, so after a due time they were re-united.

All went well for a few weeks, then one night Edwin staggered home and when Sally made a criticism, he beat her savagely. A robot marine squad was sent to intervene within minutes but unfortunately was too late. Sally had been badly beaten and kicked. She was rushed to hospital and was tended to carefully: however, her child had suffered serious harm and died.

Sally screamed the place down; distraught and wild in her grief, she needed a sedative to control her, but even then she started again as soon as she awakened.

Edwin still had to be dealt with and many girls felt he should be executed. The Command decided not: instead, he would spend the rest of his journey in a cell in isolation for his own protection. Eventually he would return to Earth as a prisoner and face prosecution.

The mood within the ship darkened as people thought about the crime. Distrust especially of young males was constantly under discussion. Most of those frequenting the bars stopped going out to get drunk.

Sally did make a re-appearance among them several months later, but no one really knew what to say to her. She still insisted that she had been to blame. A few friends suggested she find a new partner and get pregnant again. "You will get over this experience," they said. But Sally never did recover: she committed suicide.

The news tore through the fleet and just about everyone took a careful look at their own life and liaisons. Trust was now at a premium.

Gradually life resumed, perhaps a bit muted, but spirits lifted eventually. The next meeting of the donnas was intense and not always rational, but eventually it concluded that all the young mothers needed emotional as well as physical support. A group of carers was established and – with replicant support – would oversee the birth of each child and monitor each mother constantly. Family members who would have provided such aid were still on Earth and could not therefore give aid physically. The Madonnas must provide.

Chapter Nine

The impact of these events was felt throughout the Voyaging Colonies and many were becoming introspective if not actually depressed: so much was changing in their lives.

The producers of the daily news service and the various arts programmes decided to introduce a couple of 'entertainments' into the daily schedule. One, a soap opera, would lampoon a typical lower-class underprivileged family who would face all life's trials with unfailing commonsense, sometime sad, often funny and on occasion desperate.

The second would deal with the world of political control, exploring, explaining and challenging the debates and decisions of the small Colonial Elite. The chosen presenter would need to be knowledgeable enough to mount and control the debate and with fully researched support to offer an 'outsider view'. Such programmes shown on Earth Media had become very influential.

To make an impact, the cast for these roles would be selected carefully and characters should be given time to demonstrate their talents and become viewers' favourites.

The first cast members did begin well but did not have sufficient presence to hold the audience. Gradually some of those in minor roles began to show promise. The Politics Show increasingly started to feel the impact of a young woman called Shelagh Sadique, Iranian in origin; many of her views clashed with 'free love' attitudes because she took a very strict view about the behaviour of young men in society and championed the rights of women, especially the mothers.

The family soap was much more popular with this young audience, most of whom had lived with family characters like those portrayed: the stout, bossy Dad who was nearly always in the wrong, the loving mother who was a little over-played but really the anchor to all, the children wild as they grew older, but often misunderstood, troubled or simply vulnerable to outside influences. A parade of councillors, teachers and Government interventions set up the problems and opportunities that were planned to arise. Comedy, pathos, loss and love featured almost daily.

In this casting, one young man, Robert Bolsonaro, and his supposed girlfriend Lucy Ramovitch, formed a popular couple. 'Bolly' was a fat, tubby character always in desperate trouble, but somehow bumbling on unstoppably. Lucy was simply beautiful; how could she love a fool like Bolly? There were great opportunities for some intelligent psychology and ideas. Bolly was taking on a beloved role – that of the 'common man' with Lucy as 'the maid for all seasons'. After some months these two shows became the staple daily viewing for many, of the travellers. COMAS was very interested too, looking for clues to human reaction, as usual.

Popularity? What was that? Did these playground characters show versions of themselves or were they really just fabricated personalities that would fade and disappear in time? COMAS decided she would monitor audience reactions and mood for future analysis. Her monitor watched the audience as they watched the TV but, of course, discreetly.

The men of the Navigation Institute, particularly the older ones, spoke of this fascination with play-acting with contempt; time was being wasted that could have been better used to educate and to up-skill future practices. COMAS intervened, reminding them that Folk Tales, especially within families, had traditionally been used to pass ideas, attitudes and even ambitions to its next generation in their formative and early adulthood years. This 'play-acting' was simply another version of such a process.

Privately COMAS was still trying to understand why she had been written as a female persona; perhaps by watching she too would learn why comfort and reassurance was so important in human affairs.

Chapter Ten

The presence of so many young women already fulfilling their promise to breed and raise children had definitely brought a change in the atmosphere on the NY Ark.

Many Colonists had surrendered some of their freedoms and couples were forming even among those who still believed in Free Love and free association. It just seemed more comfortable to go along with the current mood, but some new tensions arose from girls who had not found compatible friends.

After widespread discussions in the General Assembly, the leaders of the Madonna Group suggested that for at least a couple of generations it would be sensible for the males to have at least two steady relationships to provide safety and security for the future children. There were many who had reservations but eventually the motion was accepted and rules were changed.

John and Sui talked all this over and agreed reluctantly for one other woman to join them, but only on a second-wife basis, and looked amongst the Colonist Women for a friend who was already pregnant – perhaps a 'Free Love'. They eventually invited Tilda, Sui Linn's half-sister. At least they knew her.

They invited her to join them for a meal and talked freely and openly about their plan for the future. Tilda did not want to join another family with strangers and readily agreed, provided her living quarters could be kept separate.

Tilda was five years older than Sui Linn, and when the marriage of their parents had been disbanded by mutual consent, she had been the essential support for her mother during the formal divorce proceedings. Her mother Sian had been terminally ill with cancer and Tilda continued to care for her right to the end of her life.

Relations with her father had been strained during this time but Chiang Lee Linn had not ceased to support for both Sian and her child. When Chiang married again – a marriage organised by their families which meant that bride and groom had only met once before the wedding – Tilda did feel resentment against his new bride, Yusin, a sixteen-year-old maiden from Shanghai, but quickly overcame her dislike, especially when Sui – the first-born of this marriage – arrived. Tilda and Yusin actually worked together well and eventually became friends. The whole family, including several more children, later moved to San Francisco, USA, where the families had already established a viable store supplying Chinese foods to the local community. Tilda became almost a second mother to Sui and guided her carefully during the years of her learning and adolescence. They were sisters indeed, although Sui did sometimes accuse Tilda of being bossy.

The chance to enrol for the Mars Colony Venture arose because of Tilda's role as a teaching assistant at MIT: with horticultural experience and experimentation, she was a natural choice for candidate.

A very determined young woman, she was therefore quite mature in attitude and as a consequence had been heavily involved with the establishment of the Women's Institute, now called the Madonnas.

The young men and the father of her future child soon learned that Tilda expected to be treated as an equal and extended the courtesy she felt her due. She was therefore something of a daunting prospect as a mother. Her successful lovers had to be very circumspect, she soon dismissed them if they showed any sign of wandering.

Given her attitudes, independent ideas and her close love for her half-sister, it was no surprise that when offered the chance of joining a steady and enlightened man as a second wife, she accepted. John was a gentle man and a strong leader who she had liked from first acquaintance.

Such decisions were not easily made and for some did not go uncontested, especially when one of the loose males was proud of his virility and took such decisions as an insult. When Tilda was offered, one big lad – Alva Gant – claimed rights and was most disturbed when his attentions were refused.

Foolishly he tried to dominate and control Tilda, but she would not permit him such liberties. He became bitter and started to malign her at every opportunity.

Word of his behaviour soon got back to Tilda, so she confronted him publicly and reported his behaviour to the Donnas Institute. They added his name to the list of undesirables who would face repatriation to Earth at the first opportunity. He did have some friends and they eventually persuaded him to calm down and seek solace elsewhere.

His records were updated but the abuses had been noted. Shelagh Sadique had made this a cause celebre in her political review anyway: Bolly was given a role based on Arlott in which he and Lucy were at loggerheads, but to give a happy ending they were finally given permission to marry. A feature on Undesirables was mooted but finally dismissed as too divisive.

Chapter Eleven

Almost unnoticed, the Arks drifted into the orbit of Mars late one night, but of course on the next day all settlers were alert, excited and sometimes trepidatious that the long transit was over.

One by one the Arks settled into a fixed position over the area of construction. The first-wave settlers were keen to take their first steps onto the planet's surface, so they were 'suited up', given oxygen cylinders and allowed to disembark in groups of ten to view the chosen site.

Construction was proceeding according to schedule but it would be about three months before the accommodation biomes were ready for occupation. However, the leading group of engineers and an architect were on hand with demonstration mock-ups of what the site and the biomes would look like in due course.

Navigation Commanders took the opportunity to talk about plans already formulated for the future of this colony and of course all had to be recorded and transmitted to Earth. Earth services made a great deal of fuss over such 'important events'.

The Colonists themselves were quite impressed with the progress made so far, but were rather disappointed to note that they would have to stay on the Arks for some time yet. Some asked Command whether they could take up their allocated living space sooner. No, they were advised, the community must stay where they were until all units were completed.

Settlement

The time after landfall turned out to be a time of grace; the voyagers were pleased to have arrived safely, because many had entertained private doubts and concerns.

Celebrations were taking place in all the various cabin sections of the Arks and even the Commanders and Navigation staff were able to stand down. Many folk spent time gazing at the rather barren landscape, half in reverence, half in speculation. Could this space become home?

For many, the daily departure of the engineer teams and necessary support staff, like medical and housekeeping units, became a time to congregate and just watch.

The rest of the days were spent checking systems and renewing and building better or more advanced replacements against the time when all would finally land and take up residence on the surface. Time was also spent watching via the Public Service Screen as they mapped every inch of the planned site. Evenings became used for socialising, music and sex: a great aid to maintaining morale and humour. Many settlers liked music, especially Mozart, Chopin and Beethoven just to 'chill out' as the Americans termed it. The tensions eased and dating, dancing and loving resumed again.

The politicians on each Ark had their own ideas about the way this new colony should be run, but co-operation and therefore compromise had to be the underlying theme. Working together towards a common goal, they hoped to achieve a balanced society, all working for the common good. Naturally there were conflicts of interest, especially when it came to the territory allocated to each Ark community.

John and Sui breathed a sigh of relief. Sui was beginning to feel the baby move and she often invited John to lay his head on her stomach and talk to their boy. The last scam had confirmed it was to be a son. The world knew or not; it could just go away for now.

Several of the others in Married Quarters felt the same and meals together often turned into sessions during which the women compared notes. The lads were a bit sidelined and some kept harking back to the programmes and the latest decisions reached. Many soon tired of this. The plans already made must stand. The young men listened to John as an elder but then ridiculed him afterwards among themselves. The 'Old Boy' they called him and could not believe that Sui Linn, the firebrand, had chosen him.

Life ticked on by: the engineers, architects and their teams of robots and replicants were working hard to finish the first biome dormitories, and one by one the new domiciles were completed. The Colonists were shown these accommodation units daily and they could now indicate their preferences. Most folk did not care; each apartment looked the same as the others, so they were allocated a numbered space.

The unattached and not yet pregnant chose to live in halls, rather like those at a university, where they could party at will. The typical block would contain the conference rooms, the ballroom, the kitchens and the dining rooms, before linking to a separate square surrounded by the apartments for the married whom the Administrators hoped would form the stable core of society.

The Arks themselves would be grounded to form the central main block, to provide familiar and well-liked facilities for a social cultural life. Self-contained, they would also become a place of safety in the event of an emergency.

The main source of concern was the establishment of a centre for Government and Social Democracy. The Admiral and Senior Captains had held the reins of command so far but it was now the time to plan ahead.

Earthside, the Administration Centre had agreed that the Admiral should become the leader, but with only three colleagues in support he could expect dispute. The remaining Captains were expected to return to Earth and their families.

Chapter Twelve

During the first political debate, it was decided that all Colonists would be placed at the same time: there would be no favouritism, no quarrels or precedence and therefore everyone would be more secure as construction continued. They settled down to watch progress and a nightly TV presentation was scheduled for 6:30 p.m. in the main viewing room.

Weeks passed and December days rolled on. Preparations were being made to celebrate their first Christmas alone on a new world. Despite the activity, there was an observable change in the atmosphere on board. Messages of goodwill and Christmas music were being beamed at them from Mother Earth. There was a sudden realisation for everyone that an irrevocable change had come to them. A sort of yearning brought out a sombre mood of reflection.

The donnas and everyone looked anew at their chosen companions and wondered 'Will I ever know the happiness I had as a child?' John was not affected directly; he had been travelling the sea and stars for a good many years, but he could feel Sui's anxiety and Tilda was down hearted too.

To cheer everyone up he suggested a carol concert and then a pantomime: he even agreed to take a comic role for himself because someone more experienced could not be found. The idea was promulgated by the Commanders and by the Madonna Association and everyone began to make some effort.

The auditions and practice sessions caused much humour, cat-calls and criticism and even before Christmas Eve, the staged chaos and mayhem had brought much pleasure. Friendships and rivalry brought out the best in the new Colonists, much to general relief. Christmas could be fun after all.

COMAS and the AI computer once again realised the vulnerability of these human beings in their care. They seemed to have a positive need to be active or to be entertained. So programmes which required their involvements would have to be devised even if robots and replicants could have done such work better. Earth Control was so informed and surveillance increased.

The mood-swings between sadness and euphoria were unsettling.

Chapter Thirteen

Moving In

Accommodation Allocation Day finally arrived and everyone was excited; the time of choosing a home was here at last. The accommodation units were built on two levels only, like old earth maisonettes. Each was generous in proportion and included three or four bedrooms, living, dining and kitchen space. Storage space was massive with most units and cupboards built in.

Each home enjoyed either a view of the central park area or on the outer ring, distant views across the terrain of Mars. The central park area was built around the various Arks which were to provide health and medical services and all forms of community activity. Sui and John chose the outer ring.

In order to give opportunity for personal enterprise, the Ark complex also included a market where individual traders could congregate and act as a community focus. Within days, services like hairdressing, clothing fabrication and sales were set up alongside an organised repair and renovation unit and of course food stalls. All this despite the fact that catering and dining counter facilities were used by all every day. The NY ARK began to feel like a real place to which people could become attached, just like home.

Sui, John and Tilda settled and the girls began to make changes to the layout, furnishings and textiles to make themselves comfortable. One bedroom, the biggest, was set aside for the children. It had a crèche and nursery area and a replicant girl employed to take care of cleaning, washing and eventually to act

34

as a nursemaid/nanny. Gemma fitted in nicely and only required a smallish wardrobe cupboard as her base.

John needed space to set up his computer links and a quiet room for study. He chose the small fourth bedroom for this purpose.

Now nicely set up, the huge lounge complex with its distant views became the area for family time and discussions. Tilda's boyfriends seemed to find such domesticity amusing but took care not to give offence, if they were at all sensible.

Time passed, duties at the hospital resumed for Sui, for the children of the First Wave were nearing delivery. Tilda worked at the Community Farm Complex, a multi-storey greenhouse and horticultural centre. Plants for food and for experiment were raised on stages over seven floors, actually hydroponic growing spaces, under speciality lighting to ensure maximum healthy growth. Tilda was getting heavy with child and could not give her work quite as much time as she would have liked, but she was happy to be useful doing things she loved.

Sui was getting slower too – her future son demanded attention, kicking and turning sometimes at the wrong moment. Increasingly the two girls needed rest and company. Friends were easy: all the donnas were in much the same position and the tearoom service area was seldom empty.

Sui and John still spent a part of each week evening time alone to talk, discuss plans and of course make love. Tilda respected this and would stay out at some community event whenever the chance arose. Music, drinking and dancing were everyday activities in the village for there were still many exercising their freedoms.

Some needed more support than others and the Institute established pre-natal exercise and advice sessions every day. The donnas, a term now used only for pregnant women, appreciated the warmth, comfort and support provided. This was a very emotional period for those young women and relationships were often strained. Many young men were lost, torn between love, responsibility and a hankering for freedom.

These tensions only began to ease as the babies began to arrive, because most young men felt pride in achieving parenthood. The computer programmes and the service robots once again recorded the shifts in human reaction.

Tilda was brought to term first and gave birth to a beautiful girl, Emma at 7lb 2oz. Days later, Sui brought my father – Henry John Linn – to term too; at 10lb 3oz he was quite a handful. John was bursting with pride and passion – father to a boy, surrogate to a girl. Both women bathed in a sort of euphoria but they had the practical task of suckling their children and for a while John's needs and wants were secondary. The replicant attendants helped more and more.

Chapter Fourteen

John had taken maternity leave to be with Sui and his new extended family, but his programme of research still needed attention, so after about two weeks, he left the women to cope and returned to the Navigation Institute with some relief.

The Institute Commanders were consolidating their power over daily routines, allocating tasks and enforcing discipline. Some of the younger men pursuing their personal freedoms too diligently were reminded of the serious purpose behind this mission.

For some this first year had clearly been an extended trial, others found the situation in such a confined and contained society did not suit them at all. The ruling Council decided that many of these dissidents would never fulfil their original role properly. After a period of research involving individual character analysis by COMAS and its servers, each candidate was profiled and either selected or requested for further engagement. Over twenty men were regarded as unsuitable and instructed that they would return to Earth on the next flight.

Their Inaugural flight to Earth would be ready in three weeks and John was instructed to take command. He and his crew would also conduct a trading mission, negotiating with Earth for supplies and materials that were running low. This command was what he had trained for in his original role; he was not given the opportunity to refuse.

He passed the news to Sui and Tilda quietly over a meal that evening. Sui was distraught but Tilda helped to smooth things between them. Tilda, ever the practical older sister, reminded Sui that John had many other responsibilities as a middle-rank navigation officer and that they could comfort each other until his return.

He did point out that he had no choice at all; he had signed on for fifteen years once again, only weeks before the Ark voyage from Earth began. This enrolment required him to obey the commands of his Senior Officers without question. All his promotion prospects and his income depended on the way he fulfilled his duties.

"I have more responsibilities ahead and I must know that you both understand," he said. Actually, Tilda was very concerned: all the old stories about sailors and voyagers came back to her. She knew many women had had to endure long periods alone as their husbands/lovers travelled the seas of Earth. How much more isolated would she and Sui become if John returned to his previous lifestyle and started to move on in the solar system.

She tried hard to keep her fears to herself but Sui was sensitive and knew something was troubling her. Eventually after a hectic time with the children, who were behaving tediously, continually demanding attention, she finally sat down to talk things over.

In the quiet of the evening, as they prepared for bed, she sat with Sui and poured out all her worries about possible troubles ahead. Sui was quietly listening but believed that John loved her, Tilda and his new family too much to abandon them. She acknowledged that he did feel the pull of the stars but this had become lessened by his new responsibilities. He would voyage in the future, but she was sure he would never go away for years (perhaps months, yes!) but she and Tilda acting together could easily manage while he satisfied his wanderlust.

They, his wives, had great ambitions and any short absences by John could be used to boost and enhance their own studies. John was human: the demands on him were intense and during these early years such cares would take their toll. He needed them to be strong, raise the kids well and maybe bolster him in times of trouble. A sound useful task lay before them.

Chapter Fifteen

In fact it was more than useful, for they both got involved again with problems in their working life. Sui found that some women were birthing their children easily – with help of course – but that a few had recently had a hard time with breached births. The practice was growing for birth by caesarean surgery: the robot surgeons were especially skilled in this. Sui wondered if some alternative, more natural technique could be used instead. She decided to research Earth records for instructions on manual turning, which was common practice by veterinary teams dealing with cows and sheep.

Having gathered advice, she asked for the opportunity to carry out this procedure. The mother, Lena Marco was not keen but wanted to see if her child could be turned enough before lockdown, to enable her to give birth naturally. In the ensuing manipulation, the stress on her vaginal muscles was quite severe but was carefully monitored by the anaesthetist, and the child, a boy, was delivered in a birthing pool some hours later. Everyone, especially Lena, was overjoyed although her condition had to be monitored carefully for three days afterwards.

Discussions within the Medical Centre went on for weeks; COMAS had recorded every detail of the procedure as well as Sui's hand movements as she turned the baby and watched this repeatedly alongside similar evidence from the Veterinary College records supplied by Earth. The verdict was perhaps inevitable: the technique might be useful and could be used to adjust position but only with consent of the mother and even then only under supervision. It did not, therefore, become common practice. After some weeks of rest, Sui next turned her attention to injections and virus controls – her curiosity knew no bounds. Fortunately the children, Emma and Henry John, were restless, often fractious and needed lots of attention. She asked for and received help from specialist replicant nurses and settled to her role as mother.

Tilda was nonetheless a bit piqued that Sui was often absent and tied up with her current project and one day made her feelings known.

Sui was patient and listened carefully to Tilda's moans but then explained why she was so intensively involved at work. Tilda realised she was being a bit unreasonable and apologised.

Privately, in her room and once again dealing with demands from the kids, she still smouldered a bit.

Relations were a little tense between the sisters for a few days, but John did not really seem to be too aware; both women tried hard to keep him happy. They might even have been a little too attentive, but he just basked in their loving attention.

Preparing for the first shuttle service demanded more and more of his time. Any oversights in planning might have serious consequences later, so reluctantly John started to work hard every day commissioning the newly built cargo vessel. John and his two deputies, Ari and Jehan Ivan, had their attention drawn to any area of difficulty by the robotic teams, usually accompanied by suggestions from Engineering Control.

Days passed in haste. To get around the need to carry passengers (the unsuitable ones), changes had to be made to convert cargo space into living quarters. Dormitory facilities did not cause problems – John simply reverted to old Naval tradition and organised hammocks and duffle-bag storage systems.

To ensure reasonably comfortable sleep he organised the dormitory in the most remote cargo hold, away from the noise and vibration. Ablution facilities, toilets, washing and shower facilities were installed but could be easily dismantled after the initial voyage. A Marine Robot Officer was also activated, with responsibility for passenger discipline on board, and was linked directly with COMAS so he could be given precise instruction in the event of trouble. John had planned for such a problem, so a small force of soldiery and sex replicants to service every man was activated, and COMAS issued very specific commands to control the activities and reactions of his team. It was all quite generous under these circumstances.

The only task left by the end of the second week was to recruit the small team to command the deck. John chose his men carefully. Few serving men would have such an opportunity to return to Earth before the end of their period of service, unless this trading activity proved a success, and he did not want to have to face desertions. Aria and Jehan were offered first refusal: both accepted.

The departure day arrived, John said his goodbyes and the cargo vessel Nancy was launched without ceremony. Sui and Tilda stayed home rather than attend: it was enough that they had to part company, even for a short time.

Chapter Sixteen

'Nancy' was fleet of foot, as her maglev systems had been designed to lower journey times. The increase in velocity was noticeable and this much lighter ship made the journey to Earth in just ten weeks – amazing, really.

She was received in a blaze of glory despite the group of failed candidates, who had in any case been dropped at Moon base before dispersal and their return home. The TV and internet stations demanded everyone's attention and soon the world knew the faces of the human crew and the vessel's Commander. Government bodies and senior businessmen all demanded their attention.

John decided enough was enough and insisted discussions about supplies begin immediately. Acting upon his own initiative, he set up a trading company in New York and engaged several men and women to run this office. Of course the AI control systems would still be slaved to COMAS with real-time links to Mars.

He and the command crew even took a week of break-time, visiting recreation facilities and some earthside holiday sites. He also made a point of contacting his only living relative, his older brother Simon, who still lived in Falmouth UK with his wife Una and a daughter. Simon as the eldest son had inherited all the family lands.

Back on duty, purchasing supplies and selling the rare minerals and essences that they had brought from Mars took a longish time. The main difficulties revolved around getting value for money spent, for although John had been given funds and would control sales personally, these monies were still limited. The Navigation

Institute would review all such trading activities with great diligence and attention to detail.

Actually John became quite annoyed over the protracted negotiations. He was much more interested in making contact with the scientific community and the universities. Some of the elements and mincrals from Mars were very rare or even non-existent on Earth and much research would be needed before their value and utility could be established. Co-operation would be essential and the free transfer of knowledge was expected by scientists at least.

Four months later, much of the furore had died down, the buying had ben completed and delivery and loading was done. John asked for and received permission to return to Mars and took off immediately. He had kept in regular contact with Sui and Tilda but was eager to get back 'home'.Arrival at Mars caused little ceremony. John was instructed to leave the cargo ship in orbit where all contents would all be analysed and de-contaminated before delivery to the Colony stores. John was given two weeks' leave and instructed to return to HQ after this period for de-briefing. Homecoming was wonderful: Sui, Tilda, the children in arms, the house servants and Gemma welcomed him like a conquering hero. COMAS and the Lares were on duty too. How could he ever wish to depart from them again?

This honeymoon atmosphere continued day after day, with hours and even days spent describing the beauties of Earth, the satellite cities and telling the family about the new trading company. John knew he would face the same sort of inquisition when he returned to HQ, so he rehearsed all he might wish to mention.

The women grew very serious as his leave period ended and reported that there had been a lot of adverse comment about John during his absence, mainly suggesting he had taken advantage of this opportunity to promote himself rather than the New Colony. This media coverage had undoubtedly been picked up by the Institute Command. He was sure about this, because his first re-connection meeting by telelink had been distinctly cool.

Chapter Seventeen

Back to work as instructed, John's first day was spent entirely in conference with the Admiral and all nine Ark Commanders. The morning session was dedicated to cargo analysis, finance and the transfer of payments. An item in John's quarters had not been listed as cargo and these officers demanded to know his reason for holding it as personal belongings.

John explained that this item was a new experimental survival suit and had been given to him by the Maglev Corporation as a gift. It was claimed by them to prolong survival under adverse conditions for nearly four days.

"Why a personal gift?" they asked.

"Why not?" he replied.

"You should have declared it anyway," they said. "What else did you get? Money, bribes, personal favours?"

John did not like the way this questioning was proceeding and said so.

"You know full well that every detail of talks and negotiations was recorded by COMAS and its servers," he said, "as well as being under permanent surveillance by Earth services. Ask them!"

The meeting adjourned.

During lunch his old boss, ARK Commander NY Frederick Bertini made a point of joining his table. Fred asked John to be patient and careful because most of the Senior Commanders believed that the media speculation about John's motives had been correct.

They had as a group failed to consider how Earth might regard the leader of the First Trade Mission and regretted their oversight.

He should not expect an easy interview after lunch but must hold his temper.

The atmosphere at the afternoon session was tense even before the de-briefing started. They let him read his report and give his thoughts and reasoning about future trading but then began a barrage of more personal questions:

Was he aware of the allegations of personal self-aggrandisement?

How did he see his role as a Navigation Officer and as a Colonist developing? Surely a rather unique combination.

Why had he set up the IMARCO Trading Office without specific instructions? What was its role and status? Was it under Mars control or his personal vehicle for future trade?

Why did Earth media consistently refer to him as John Fisher ,CEO Mars? He had no such status nor authority to give such an impression. John answered as quietly and honestly as he could, but saw that Mars Commanders were seething with jealousy and bitterness. He was dismissed.

John's wives were anxious and could hardly wait to hear the outcome of the de-briefing session and it took several days to calm them and give re-assurance privately. In the quiet of his own study, he recalled the sequence of events and was not certain about his future; nonetheless, he kept these doubts to himself. What was done could not be undone.

Back at his work station on deck, he took time to review the reports and play back the records of the interview, but could not find any serious fault with his performance.

About a week after his landing, COMAS reported that the Maglev Corporation had called to ask if John had tested the survival suit: they would welcome any information and comments he had to make. John sent a thank you note and commented that he would test the suit as soon as he could find some free time, but this was not likely to occur for several months yet.

NASA base had also made contact; they had received a request from MIT for evaluation of a defensive weapon designed to give warning of unusual emissions of particles from our Sun. They asked permission to land the equipment and site it on Mount Olympus.

John was rather embarrassed and instructed COMAS to pass this request to the Admiral and the Senior Navigation Team. He was called upon almost immediately to explain and evaluate this request. He gave the idea full support but the Starlight Team were clearly antagonistic and even more suspicious than ever.

The coolness he felt whenever he returned to his workstation continued and he realised that all his communications with Earth were under surveillance.

Weeks passed in uncomfortable isolation but gave him time to look through the record of his satellite and debris research and note one or two interesting possibilities. He gave COMAS instructions to intercept this debris, enslave it and pull it to the surface of Deimos for inspection and analysis.

Finally, the tension in the atmosphere at Navigation Central was becoming unacceptable and Navigation Command called a meeting. John was advised that his future role had been re-evaluated.

Command now believed a serious error had been made when the Command Captain on the NY ARK had permitted him to marry a young woman from the Colony First Wave recruits, but at the same time allowed him to retain his privileged status as a Navigation Officer. The present view was that as a consequence John had been permitted to gain status in the future Colony with this unique combination, which could cause much trouble in the future.

A decision had been reached. He could not leave his Colony commitments – he now had two wives and several children to raise. Consequently his appointment as a Navigation Officer was cancelled immediately. His pension rights and a redundancy were safe and he could expect to receive a decent settlement within four weeks. They thanked him for his service and he was dismissed. He went home to his wives.

Chapter Eighteen

The news of John's dismissal caused quite a stir in the Second Officers' ranks; some who had liked the idea of finding love among the colonists thought again and decided to return to Earth instead. The captains felt the same impulse – these men were seasoned travellers and a life of relative idleness on Mars or a long stay as politicians did not appeal to most.

One of the consequences of this disruption was a reduction in the numbers involved in Starlight Command. The Admiral in charge was appointed governor of Mars Colony for five years and at the end of that time would return to Earth for his retirement. He did need to keep a support team to help him administer the Colony, but his cabinet would only consist of two officers and perhaps a similar number of aides. All other posts would be filled by Colonists or AI guides.

Starlight Navigation Centre gradually emptied as the returning officers took flight for Earth to continue their careers and other plans. COMAS and her servers monitored all this displacement activity and filled up the space with replicants under their command.

Many of the Colonists with perhaps an ambition for leadership took full notice of these opportunities, which would impact upon Colony life in the near future. Two families took steps to position their children into Politics and Economics courses in anticipation.

The ambitious were the Rosenblums and the Ambignales, COMAS took note and provided details of opportunities at Earth Institutes of Learning if required.

Both these families were headed by determined women. Julia Rosenblum was the great-granddaughter of one of the founders of Chase Manhattan Bank, in New York. The family ,originally refugees from Europe, had worked hard, traded successfully and had eventually become a part of the International Association of Jewry. She always observed the rules of her religion and had a strong hold on both her husband, Reuben, and her sons. Her ambitions for her two sons Isaac and David knew no bounds. If this Colony succeeded, she believed her son Isaac should lead it.

Maria Ambignale came from a successful wine-growing and producing family of Spanish/Mexican descent. Her father and brothers still farmed a huge vineyard in the Napa Valley. Wine from this vineyard was stored carefully and available for sale, so money was steadily accumulating. Maria thought that women should take control of family affairs and direct the efforts of all boys and girls. She was keen to promote the interest of her second daughter Angelina who, though no angel, was very like her mother.

So, there were two North American families of immigrant origin who felt it was their God-given right to rule. Both families were in strong financial positions and could send their children to the finest colleges on Earth to further their ambitions.

The husbands, Reuben Rosenblum and Carlos Ambignale, were quite good friends but the rivalry between the women brought them a lot of strain and caused upset at times.

John became concerned; so far most Wave Communities had opted for an open society where all lived and worked together, but as the days and weeks passed, each of the nine Ark Villages started to experience competition between individuals and families.

He had been accused of this himself following his mission to Earth and believed that envy was the primary cause. No matter how communities tried to blend and share, some were bound to do better than average while others would take advantage of temporary distinctions, such as higher status work, more money and wealth or greater physical strength and endeavour to maintain that position.

COMAS reported that, like the Rosenblums and the Ambignales in the NY village, each of the Wave communities were growing such separations. Three of these lordly families could in the future be expected to compete for powers: the Chiangs, the Morgans and the Lees. Perhaps not so surprising, the Bolsonaros might also compete – not 'Bolly' but definitely his brother Eduardo. Others would in time rise to compete without any doubt at all. In a place and at a time when all are considered equal, some humans will always claim superior status and privilege.

COMAS made it clear that her psychological studies showed such changes were inevitable in human society. The only possible counter was free access to education and equality of opportunity for all.

Chapter Nineteen

Surprisingly the atmosphere within the Colony Village sweetened; many were sorry to see John humiliated and went out of their way to welcome him and his wives when they came amongst them. Perhaps all these changes had made people think and make up their own mind about his intentions, rather than rely on official views.

The donnas went to extraordinary lengths to welcome Sui and Tilda at the next meeting. Tilda was even invited to talk about the supply of food and report on the working of the Agriculture Team.

John himself was quite confused – what could he engage himself in now that his main occupation had ended? Sitting in his study and reviewing his options quietly, he started to realise that he had achieved a freedom of action that he had never known before. He could work and become anything or do anything within his physical capabilities. To start, he re-connected his computer links to COMAS and picked up his old satellite research, which had not been deleted.

Sui and Tilda were relieved: family life could restart again. They suggested that he spend at least one or two hours a day at leisure activities with other Colony men, for John had not taken part in such social activities so far. John took this advice and did make an effort to mix for a while.

Gradually the tendency to work alone reasserted itself, so he began to study geology and terrain records in the surrounding land mass. His experimental support suit from Maglev became very useful because it extended his range of coverage and the time to spend outside the camp complex The nearby Marinas Trench was fascinating and the Rift Valley Walls showed the physical history of Mars development. How many thousands of years would pass before such an alien environment could become home? The terraform team welcomed his interest as COMAS started to offer a chance to study geology, physics and chemical analysis and assigned a dedicated AI programme to assist in his education. Life was picking up pace.

Sui and Tilda noted the change and over a few days began to introduce family matters back into their discussions at leisure times. During his long absences the sisters had talked about their life together and Tilda had taken the opportunity to ask if Sui would permit her to conceive and raise one or two children with John.

She was bored with the macho male set and wanted the chance to conceive children with promise. Sui was shocked but gradually began to see the sense of such a change. John would probably need to agree to diversify his family structure in this way, but he would then have regular sex with two females who were already united and directly linked to each other. The family and especially the children would gain a lot from such security. The seed of good men should not go to waste.

After a long period of discussion – mainly about jealousy, rivalry and regularity – John agreed. He was quite content with his loving relationship with Sui and did not want this impaired. Sui agreed but her sister was a loving woman too and needed occasional sex. Any children born to her would automatically become part of the family and it might be beneficial for these to be part of the same inheritance, thus united.

Days passed but then Sui made arrangements to take the children to the Village Crèche for a few hours. Tilda and John took the hint and retired to bed.

Their first lovemaking was active: Tilda had not had sex for some weeks and she was very eager to 'get on with it'. John slipped in beside her and she rolled him over and swallowed his penis, pulling him gently.

"No," he said, "take it more slowly."

So she stopped, opened her legs and pushed his penis into her vagina. Tilda moaned with pleasure as he penetrated deeper and she began to buck and ride him furiously until they climaxed.

They stayed still for a good while and then John touched her breasts, stroking her body and legs, slowly leading to high arousal. Tilda came again rather noisily. They talked and caressed for a while and then departed to shower and dress again.

Sui was desperate to learn about his first session, but all John would say was that Tilda was very active. It took her days of wheedling before Tilda would answer her questions. Tilda said it had been good but thought John was rather quiet compared to her wildest boys: she was used to harder action. Nonetheless, petting had been wonderful and she looked forward to her next visit.

Sui herself was ready too and that night she and John enjoyed a really long slow session, much to the satisfaction of them both.

The wives were both keen to try again but John insisted they wait for a few days so he could recover. Coping with two eager girls might be fun but certainly draining.

During their next liaison John insisted that Tilda let him lead. He explored her body thoroughly, touching and stroking her until she reached a pitch of desire and then entered her gently as he rode to climax. She definitely liked this and was pleased even more when he was aroused again some minutes later. This was going to be fun, she thought.

Next day Sui was again eager to talk and took delight in learning that Tilda was slowing but really enjoying herself. She had always thought John a very competent lover. One result was that after a busy day in the field Sui demanded her 'rights' again. Boy did she mean it and he thought "Wow, I had better start on an intense fitness programme or I'll be lost."

This passionate second honeymoon soon brought results: both wives were now pregnant, but still remained *keen*.

Chapter Twenty

John was getting restless again. He definitely liked being married and raising his family but needed more time to attend to his own interests and continue his studies. He made contact with the climate team and asked for permission to visit for a study period. Permission was given without demur and COMAS started a review of the sitc at Webbland and gave details of the current stage of progress.

Far to the south, a crater of about five kilometres in circumference was being 'shielded', provided with a closed 'watery climate' and had been studded with lichens, moss and Earth-style fenland plants. There were no results so far but it was a promising start.

John told his wives over dinner that evening and they both laughed.

"Need a break, John?" said Sui.

"Yes indeed," he replied.

In any event Sui now faced her final medical examination, and if successful could hang out her shingle as a qualified doctor of medicine, specialising in natural disciplines.

Tilda frowned. "I suppose that means you expect me to look after the babies," she said.

"Yes please," they replied. "Gemma will help."

In truth all she had to do was tell them interesting stories and give them a cuddle, so it was no bother really. Gemma did the rest.

The raised plateau area known as Webblands according to Schiaparelli, was broken terrain raised high above a feature he had called the Maraldi Sea and John was keen to view this area where once great waters had flowed. Seas were one of the key areas for re-wilding, if enough water could be freed to flow again during the summer months.

The following week, John kissed his wives goodbye, stepped into his survival suit, boarded his transporter sled and left. As he exited the village biome through the airlock, he felt a quiet relief: he was happiest on the move and most of his life, until Sui arrived, had been nomadic.

Overnight he stopped at the tip of a small cave complex high in the hills, lay back and watched the night sky until he slept. Up early with changing light and the distant Sun low in the sky, he swiftly traversed the small final amount of terrain to reach Webb. He was welcomed by the team over breakfast.

The site leader, Indira Khan, introduced the team at the table, then all adjourned for the briefing. Sussie Lamm explained that the crater chosen was used because the original impact of a meteorite had been massive, causing huge damage and containing sufficient heat to fuse the surface around the impact point. The debris left on the surface of the crater also fused to create a small central raised peak, now their base.

Jane Shapiro then covered the basin flooding, which was achieved by heating part of the ice lagoon one thousand metres below the surface and feeding this into the crater. She explained that this phase had only been completed in the last month. First the engineer Simon Clay Johnson and his robot team had had to construct a shielding web to cover the whole site, power it by solar generators and adjust the balance of the atmosphere and gravity.

The naturalist Rahul Khan, Indira's husband, was trying to create a marshland environment before introducing his 'Siberian' mosses and this had been achieved by adding soil, human and animal wastes and shredded packing cases and anything to give his plants chance to survive. In the last four days a sort of slime had formed a shape, and air bubbles were making a small disturbance on the surface occasionally. The whole team was very enthused by this and the mood generally was optimistic. Anaerobic analysis might help.

John was the first visitor they had received since reporting start-up to HQ, but they wondered what had brought him to visit. Were they under inspection?

"No," said John and explained that he had wanted to escape shutdown and find an untrammelled view of the skies above this remote site.

He told them that if his presence would disturb them, he would leave immediately. They all said "No! Please stay," but privately were intrigued by his solitary initiative. Isolation for its own sake… *unusual*, they thought.

In fact they were not correct. John might be without human company but his communication unit was directly limited to COMAS and he could talk to his wives, his fellow colonists and even colony management whenever he wished. They in turn could follow him in real time if the need arose.

His studies of the physical structure of Mars and any surrounding debris had commercial interest too, especially if the Colony was to become independent of Earth and gather wealth and influence eventually.

For this moment in time, the New Wave Colonists were somewhat independent, relying on robots, AI and engineered solutions to cope with a formidable alien environment. If tetra-forming should ever become a reality and prove sustainable, other human nations and groups would want their share of any benefits and territorial rights would be disputed.

John intended to map the surface of the planet and all its known potentials so that his Colony could consolidate its hold, thus benefitting future generations. COMAS knew his purpose and even approved: foresight, ambition and perseverance were very desirable traits in a trail-breaking leader.

John had soon realised that a future Earth like Mars was unlikely. Only Earth was really home to mankind and he would have to consider the future rationally, if only for the sake of the family. These next few weeks would give him time to observe progress on one project and ponder his future course of action.

He returned home, slowly landing at points of interest for a day or two to carry out a personal inspection. He noted and recorded the presence of mineral deposits likely to prove useful in future times.

Chapter Twenty-One

When he finally arrived back at the village, he was welcomed with enthusiasm by both women, who were now big with children, but he felt that all was not as smooth and easy as he would like. After several days accepting the occasional fit of pique and sideways comments, he sat down with Sui and Matilda to learn the reasons for this tension.

Slowly at first but then in an outpouring of grief, they explained that they had each faced personal hostility from friends and neighbours. It was made clear to them that many in the New Colony were very suspicious and worried by John Henry's frequent solitary expeditions. He had a reputation as a loner, but many felt he was deliberately keeping his distance from the common herd in order to establish himself and his family as superior and therefore as an exclusive group of leaders: kings, princes and lords of Mars. The memories of the media's report from Earth did not offer any rebuttal of this idea.

John needed to spend some time building trust and a relationship with at least some of the New Wave families. He sighed and after a few days decided that he would have to step out of the shadows and let his fellow Colonists into his confidence; also he must take on more public duties.

The first thing he did was to book a session at the planetarium and then set up a full geogramme of the Mars terrain, with detailed analysis of certain features with potential by COMAS and her servers. He would then offer an open discussion to explain his views, give his explanations of possible alternatives and answer questions. He posted a notice on the Village website and daily TV services, setting this contact for one week hence.

The response was overwhelming, COMAS reported that every seat at the planetarium had been booked. The ruling Junta had taken places and the leaders of all the Ark villages were invited to visit personally, together with their advisors, of course. All NY Village families planned to attend and TV and other media from Earth would record the programme in full.

John realised that his wives had been right: everyone wanted to see him, hear him and of course judge him for themselves He was now very concerned; so much depended upon the outcome, not least for his own family. The wives gave him special attention, cosseting him, fending off visitors and all communications, so that he could give all his attention to planning his presentation. He talked of Earth links and his view that trading and financial support would be needed for some generations yet. But he took special care to create a view about future prosperity and value to mankind, both as an asset and a stepping stone to future explorations.

He ended with music: Gustav Holst's Planets Suite naturally. The audience reaction was stunned silence for quite a time – to John it seemed forever – then slowly, steadily the applause began and then accelerated to a thunderous roar. Mankind at full throttle… WOW!

John was relieved that his public speaking was over and quietly returned home exhausted and a little overcome by the reception he had been given.

He sat looking out of the window in the lounge area, pleased to be watching nothing but shifting sands and changing colours as the short days passed. The wives and the children let him rest.

After a few days he began to read again and then turned to COMAS for an update and reviewed all that has passed.

He was quite surprised to note how calm and controlled he appeared when speaking (but this certainly did not show how he had been feeling) and some of his residual tensions eased.

One section of the COMAS report had sparked his interest. It was only a brief comment from one of the replicant controllers under COMAS command who wrote:

'Although the idea and plans put forward by John Fisher were lucid and comprehensive, he did not comment on the status and employment of the replicants under your control. We were a little disappointed; the replicants are complex human-like creations designed to intelligently take the place of humankind when exploring alien territory. We are currently used to provide sex and services on Mars and consider this to be a limited use of our true potential.'

John thought they certainly had made an intelligent case for consideration here and at some time in the distant future. "I must look seriously at the ways we employ these people," he said to himself. "Did I say people? They are certainly more like us than any other servants, and obviously politically-minded."

Chapter Twenty-Two

This presentation set in motion so many changes in administration that the Colonist began to yearn for certainty. The world and every agency ran stories about the Fisher family of Cornwall, many of whom had been fishermen, sailors and boat builders. There were even several claims to fame. One Anne Fisher, a barge-builder's daughter, had once plied the Thames daily as a ferrywoman. She became well known and even became a member of the Watermen and Lightermen Guild.

Another relative had crowned a naval career as Admiral of the Fleet, keen on promoting and improving the world-renowned Royal Navy during the early twentieth century.

John's career also came into focus with a number of ex-RN men coming forward to offer tales and anecdotes.

John and his wives realised he could no longer live a quiet nomadic existence. He had become and would now remain the 'voice of the Mars colony', willing or not.

Two months later, John was called to attend a meeting at the Navigation Institute. The Admiral explained he and the remaining Ark Captains had been instructed to disband and return to Earth. Earth had asked John to take up the role of First Minister and form a government.

This was not some scatterbrain adventure, led by wild and unruly venturers who needed to be controlled and directed in military fashion. Mankind wanted to establish a community and eventually perhaps a new off-world base from which further exploration of the solar system and Deep Space could be launched.

Failure would set such plans at nought and might eventually mean fallback and decline. The presence, by chance of a man steady enough to help a people, must be encouraged in every way possible.

Of course John Fisher would never hear of their reasons for making this offer, but with luck would be given new impetus by this vote of confidence.

The Admiral and his team knew nothing of theses deliberations but as Serving Officers, would proceed as instructed, reluctant or not. They looked forward to a comfortable retirement after being involved with this venture for nearly four years. Quite enough, they thought, and left with few regrets. Many breathed a sigh of relief.

John was now faced with the prospect of leading the Colony as it edged on to becoming a well-integrated and hopefully science-based economy. Where the hell could he find some help?

The answer of course, was COMAS: her database was stuffed with a thousand years of ideas culled from the countries of Earth. Though not always successful, these ideas could show him one of the ways to proceed.

The news spread quickly throughout the Colony and the more ambitious came to offer support and their loyalty in days ahead. Others, perhaps more indifferent or envious, accepted the change with some scepticism. Fisher could succeed or fail, in which case they and the families would have to take over themselves, an exciting prospect for some.

One thing was certain; withdrawal of the Navigation Commanders would or should bring a relaxation of tensions. No one would be reporting regularly on their activities and even if COMAS recorded these, control would remain local.

John Fisher and his family could be approached directly and the more caring or organised families could add pressure to ensure some advantage for them and theirs.

The Fishers would give the lead as they had since the adventures began, but this did not mean that control passed entirely to that family. John was well aware of these new pressures and talked with Sui and Tilda, suggesting caution and restraint should be exercised in any dealing with the Madonna and the Matriarchy. This period of changeover might prove a time of great tension.

Their quiet self-interested existence might need to be suspended until this trial period ended, perhaps even until he himself felt able to retire and surrender power.

The wives were quite supportive and would help if they could but realised the planning, reorganising and consolidation of power would have a major impact on John and family life.

John's earthside colleagues were pleased, as Prime/First Minister John would now resume Control of IMARCO. He was the founder of this trading company and could be expected to promote its business and influence.

Chapter Twenty-Three

Sui and Tilda, now effectively the 'first ladies 'of Mars, soon held a reception and dance for their friends .John realised his enhanced status brought additional responsibilities.

He asked all the Village leaders to submit the names of at least two individuals who would be willing to serve as members of the Government and join him at Institute HQ in two weeks' time.

There was nothing more he could do for now and he took off for a long weekend alone. Eventually, he ended up back at Webblands and was received with warmth by his friends on the team. Home on the following Tuesday, he settled into quiet contemplation and thought. The wives loved him and left him to settle.

Both were being good because their babies were stirring strongly and they needed rest themselves. A new replicant nursemaid had been added to the team and Gemma was now very busy talking, singing and starting lessons with the children. One of them, Emma Linn, was beginning to show signs of musical talent – much to the pleasure of her parents. So the wives sang lullabies as they worked.

Now, as his 45th birthday approached, John looked around him. How life had changed: married twice over, four youngsters and two more to be added soon and now the full responsibility for the creation of a just New Society. He ought to be feeling exhausted but instead he could hardly wait for the first Parliamentary Session.

COMAS reported that all nine communities had nominated representatives; each had been examined and their potential had been considered satisfactory. The first session with John and his team of advisors had been scheduled and would take place on Friday 1st May – the following week – and the Auditorium at the

Navigation Institute was being prepared. The restaurant and dining rooms were given a gloss and drinks and snacks and communal dining catered for. All was now ready for this historic occasion.

The day came inevitably; as Deimos slid over the morning sky, the delegates and representatives arrived, settled and awaited the opening speeches and ceremonies. In this their expectations were dashed. John entered the hall, took his place and started to talk through his programme straight after welcoming all.

As First Minister, John would serve for a maximum term of fifteen years, the standard election term, in order to work through any snags in his proposed system. All representatives would serve five-year terms, but could stand for re-election after this period.

Then they should move on, giving opportunities to younger, fresher colleagues. No individual should serve beyond ten years even if re-elected.

He did not foresee a future in which he would continue in office either, provided a suitable successor could be found. This system would ensure that new ideas and changing priorities would find room to work.

To help each community, a course of politics, economics and psychology would be made widely available to all Colonists for those interested in such arts and or in media work. The aim was to create an educated population capable of effective debate and to overcome any hidden bias they might own.

The men and women in the Auditorium now would form the nucleus of the new system and would be offered the chance to lead and improve new state departments. John proposed the following:

Treasury, Education, Health and Medical Science, Business/Economics, Media and the Arts. Five Ministries in all, the leader of which would become a member of the Cabinet and able to influence the Prime Minister. John's own service would be in the fields of Policy and Politics.

When they had chosen where the individuals wished to serve, he would require the cabinet to nominate a Deputy PM, presumably one of the Ministers.

He had already appointed a Speaker for the House of Representatives, one Marisol Mugave, who had definite views about rules, regulations and compliance. He then brought Marisol to the forum and introduced her. They would find her a real force for good and for the preservation of independent rights. They all applauded as this formidable woman stood before them.

Cabinet meetings would take place once a month initially and then every three weeks permanently. All other contact would be through a dedicated secure internet link and recorded for future reference by COMAS and its servers.

"Now go and take lunch and discuss your initial reactions," said John. "Tomorrow at 11 a.m. we will re-convene!"

There was a great hubbub as the representatives got to their feet and stumbled out of the hall. John did not join them for lunch.

The next day the meeting was chaired by Marisol as Speaker;;she would also be leader of the house and all representatives would be under her control, at least in open forum.

She asked for nominations and four posts were accepted immediately. The two disputed offices were Treasury and Media, both seen as spheres with considerable influence. She adjourned the meeting for lunch and asked those intending to compete to follow her in private session.

She took Treasury first. She reminded all that John as First Minister would also be the overall Lord of the Treasury, that Mars was dependent entirely on Earth finance and that at this time reserves were very low. The Minister responsible for this department would need to be financially experienced and very diplomatic, personally dealing with John on a daily basis.

Next, Media: the main responsibility here would be an ability to work with Earth media, their demands and conflicts. Those news services were notoriously fickle and ever eager for news of conflict and dispute, much of which they actively promoted themselves. Who amongst the candidates felt themselves capable of handling such turmoil? She then left them to ponder and resolve their own affairs. Politics was the art of negotiation and compromise, she reminded them and suggested they report back the next day. They were satisfied: Marisol had made them think. Their candidates soon selected were rather concerned at the potential damage that might be caused to their reputations at home base, but eventually agreed to serve.

This first meeting ended harmoniously but again without undue ceremony. John suggested each Minister should return to base, familiarise him/herself with the task and the current state of their departmental affairs. He also suggested they appointed a deputy, a personal assistant and researcher and some additional bureau staff if their budget could cover this.

This would all take time if it was to be done well, but he also required some political ideas and thoughts about the shape of Mars security and its government in the future. Full use, he said, should be made of earthside political history; it had been researched, analysed and debated for thousands of years. The list of ministers was announced as follows:

1. Treasury – Eli Levine

2. Education – Cho En Mei

3. Health & Medical Science – Elsa Van Doren

4. Business & Economics – Marco Mastrione

5. Policy & Politics – Prime Minister

"To conclude," said John, "you all now have high motivation and a desire to serve. Keep to your purpose and resolve to do well. My door is permanently open to you personally during this start-up period.

Thank you all for your support and farewell. This meeting is closed."

The conference ended but almost every delegate wanted to talk, so the majority retired to the restaurant and bar, where they drank and socialised for quite a time before returning to their own Villages. Marisol joined them happily; they would need to work together on many occasions and should get to know each other. John did not join them and a few future colleagues were unhappy about this. First Minister or not, he would need their co-operation in the future.

Chapter Twenty-Four

In John's home village, some of his supporters were concerned at the delay in setting up a Central Authority; many believed he should have taken up the role of Leader and Controller immediately then sorted out matters of administration later. John was aware of this undercurrent of thinking but remained confident that the Mars Colony would benefit from his slow, considerate approach in the long term.

He had not sought power but now it was in his hands he intended to build a system as fair and just as possible. To do this he needed committed allies and the goodwill of all who had helped. Marriage and fatherhood had motivated him.

Days passed in detailed thought and research and even before the equinox he was present at the birth of two more children, Lynn Rose and Mae Linn, twins so identical that even Tilda – their house mother – had trouble in differentiating between them, until some weeks later she discovered a small starlight blemish on Lynn's shoulder.

Tilda was enchanted by them both and quite soon gave birth to a girl herself. Pink and a very quiet contented baby, they decided to call her Sophie. John now had two wives and seven children to care for and love.

His wives really needed to avoid conceiving more children for a time, or the toll on their health could be dangerous, so he set aside time the next evening to discuss conception and the use of the 'pill' before or after sex. Sui and Tilda had been thinking about this too; they asked whether he would take responsibility and wear a condom or would prefer they took responsibility. A serious discussion followed, looking at all the risks associated with these methods. The women finally decided to control fertility themselves, much to John's relief.

John began to think about the structure of this new society. Under the Captains, all decisions had been made at the Navigation Institute without consultation. He would try to shape political control on a more inclusive basis and believed in democracy, despite its many faults.

The Executive, the Prime Minister and his cabinet would rule but with full accountability to the people. The population levels at present were under ten thousand; they did not need formal representation yet, but as the society grew and drifted further apart, a formal chamber of debate would be useful. He would call this gathering of representatives just that: the House of Representatives. Each representative would be elected by future communities. He would set the term of office at ten years maximum, subject to re-election after five years.

Each *rep* would be fully accountable to his or her constituency and could be dismissed from office within three months by formal notice in writing. Combination along ideological lines would be banned, and each rep would be expected to reach a personal decision about rules and proposed laws, and vote accordingly. Laws and suchlike would have to reach a 70% level of support to become valid.

Enough to be going on with, he thought and relaxed again, joining Sui and Tilda in their daily routines and pleasures.

Chapter Twenty-Five

Eight years later, while all departments functioned well, some were still under pressure from expectations of the people. News came from Earth that the newly formed Chinese government had decided to reinforce their own influence and initiate the setting up of a Chinese population centre. They did notify John of their intentions before making their moves as an act of courtesy but did not ask for permission.

John realised that many Earth societies had similar ambitions and would monitor his reaction. He gave a warm welcome to the newcomers in prospect and offered an official welcome and reception. The content of his 'note' was intercepted and the whole media of Earth spread the news. Beijing made no reply.

Within New Wave Colony the news was not so welcome and their disquiet became even greater when COMAS and the news media reported that China had flown a whole satellite city to land at their base at Ausonia 1. This community, twenty thousand strong already, had a full complement of engineers and scientists and a general population with a working Communist Party Secretariat in full control.

Ausonia 1 communicated their desire to maintain friendly co-operation with the Wave but they said little more and would not need an official welcome. John sent his compliments.

Life might become a touch more complicated, but Ausonia 1 was nearly two thousand kilometres away. Because it was a fully integrated and working unit, Ausonia 1 had some advantages but it also had problems too. The Chinese population had not been pre-selected. It had already become a place of residence, work and living space for a whole stratum of society before being sent to Mars. Consequently the people arriving had all the old perceptions and attitudes that had so influenced Earth. In this sense it was not a new society but a copy of an older one. Quarrels, disputes and dissatisfactions with the status quo had all arrived on Mars too. John decided to request permission to establish an Embassy at Ausonia 1, but his request was rejected.

COMAS made John aware that there had already been several attempts to breach security. She had forestalled these so far, but the quantity and the quantity of the hacker approach showed so far that these attempts had only been exploratory. COMAS had taken the chance presented to plant markers and telltales into the Chinese systems, but she expected these to be identified and removed or frustrated quite quickly.

She, her servers and analysts would now pay attention to their own defensive shields. John thanked COMAS for her support. He would have to try again and again to build trust with the Government of that city.

After considerable deliberation, John decided to tackle this situation directly. He discussed his ideas with COMAS and Marisol, proposing that he offer free unhindered access to all Wave Records, especially those of scientific interest. In exchange he would ask for reciprocity from Ausonia 1. All involved were dubious, earthside prejudices very much on their mind. earthside controllers were similarly unimpressed, so John explained in great detail. He wanted to aim for a stable world where information and ideas could be shared by all. The environment of Mars was dangerous enough to human life without allowing bickering and conflict to arise in the New Colonies. He fully realised that Chinese leaders at Ausonia 1 might reject this idea of co-operation, but he intended to make his offer on TV and the internet with full publicity both on Mars and Earth.

An interesting idea which might act as a catalyst even if rejected. The listeners were very divided but as usual did not want to be seen as die-hards and reactionaries. So, he would proceed in the full understanding that any adverse consequences would be attributed to him.

John knew this anyway and ran a full programme of persuasion, with explanations of his reasons, his personal analysis of the situation and a discussion about possible consequences. The Media everywhere were excited and ran this day after day with many Authorities and Celebrities offering comments, both for and against.

The silence from Ausonia 1 and Beijing was quite tangible, A Chinese society has seldom acted in haste and in any case it was certain they believed their own science and intelligence base was considerably superior to that available to the New Wave Colonists.

One definite response was the arrival of another Satellite City, India's Maharastra 1. But this new group gave full warning and politely held formal celebrations, to which all were invited.

Chapter Twenty-Six

The arrival of the Satellite Cities had definitely changed the balance of power within the Mars Colony. Quiet and often insular at first, the central authorities controlling these population centres gradually experienced a lessening of control from earthside.

This was inevitable, for although communication links were good, they were not spontaneous – simply a matter of time over distance. Decisions regarding daily life, targets and even supply of necessities had to be taken locally.

As a consequence, trade between the cities and the Wave community began to increase, meaning that lines of communications between settlements had to be opened and improved as swiftly as possible. It also meant – even in these days of robotic service – contact between individual humans.

Quite quickly the barrier to trade between Maharastra and Wave were breached, for the Indian merchants had traded with the west for generations, long before conquest by Great Britain. Many of its people had continued to work for their former rulers and had even developed spices, foods and services specifically for European markets.

The Chinese at Ausonia 1 continued to be insular, which was hardly surprising, as one of the oldest human societies on Earth. Such was their diligence that success had been inevitable.

Modernising at great pace, the Chinese had gathered information and intelligence from every source available in many areas of business, and were renowned for creating silks, teas and gunpowder. Their skill in handicrafts, art and sculpture was revered throughout modern society. Even here on Mars they had made great strides in designing solar clothing, footwear and transport. John was therefore very keen to establish trading links whenever possible.

Gradually, very gradually, he was recognised as a possible client and eventually he was invited to attend a major Internal Trade Fair at Ausonia 1.

The Chinese Controller intended that John should be impressed and he was. Their version of the Maglev sled could be either a plain workshop cargo carrier or a wealthy person's prestige carriage. They also used a camping structure for visits to mining sites or for venturing into the frozen wastelands, easily erected and moveable.

This, which they called a yurt, packed into a relatively small case, but at the touch of a battery-powered button would inflate a ribbed structure, covered with a resilient photovoltaic outer cover, which would gather solar energy sufficient to power lighting, heating and a workshop. The single-entry point was a decent size and was enclosed by airlocks. The inner lock had to be closed before the outer lock could be opened.

John immediately made an attempt to buy one of these tents but was refused. The Chinese considered this yurt a valuable asset and had no intention of sharing the technology.

The traders at the show were very apologetic but the rules laid down by Centre must be obeyed. They did, however, promise that some trading activity between Ausonia 1 and Wave would be permitted if it was considered to be mutually beneficial. Not now of course, but one day soon. Rather disappointed, John returned to the Wave Village with nothing to offer his group. But first contact had been made. Time – especially when dealing with Chinese bureaucracy – was long and elastic.

Chapter Twenty-Seven

Soon it was time to call the next executive meeting for the Autumn Session in September. Surprisingly, this went smoothly, each appointed Minister wanting to make a good impression. Term Three would be interesting.

The first to speak, Eli Levine for Treasury, took a measured approach, giving precise details of the present state of the Colony's financial position and its reserves. He follows this by talking of the known expenses over the next twelve months and suggested ways finance could be brought in by borrowing in London and New York, provided the Prime Minister approved.

The others followed this lead and some of the reviews caused concern. Colony affairs had certainly not received the care that was needed and every remedy would require financing properly.

Each Minister had prepared a written report and included a brief review of the things which could be improved. John was pleased with this action and that professional help with the next series of meetings could be arranged. It also seemed clear that some sort of Professional Civil Service Bureau was needed on a permanent basis. Perhaps an appointed Cabinet Secretary could take the lead in the recruitment drive. The Minister agreed.

The meeting ended smoothly. COMAS was instructed to advertise for a Cabinet Secretary across Mars and Earth media services. NY office would handle interviews and offers of help.

John now had something of a dilemma on his hands; he had not wanted to create a massive Government bureaucracy. He had assumed the Ministers could not only formulate ideas about how to run their department but also implement and put in motion the changes they felt necessary in the organisations under their control.

Clearly now he had asked too much of these men and women. He could install replicant and robot servers to help but he would need leadership by humans to give his team support.

The youthful population of the Wave Village meant that commercial and practical experience was a premium. Nonetheless some individuals must possess inherited ability, so he asked COMAS to trawl the family records and see if candidates on Mars could be trained and employed in these services.

NY reported that many were interested in the Cabinet post but all had reservations about serving for life on Mars. No takers, therefore! London made a similar report.

So should he revise his plans? Yes! He asked Marisol and one woman, Ellie Magellan, CEO at the hospital in charge of community health programmes, to join him. Ellie had been a vociferous critic when any matter regarding public health was being talked about. She had built a strong team and Sui had frequently mentioned her in conversation. She clearly had a good knowledge of Village affairs, strong leadership skills and the ability to command loyalty.

John told his colleagues of his dilemma and the lack of help from Earth. He asked for their advice and opinions about the way to overcome this difficulty.

Both women asked for two days' delay while they talked together and reviewed possible options: he agreed.

The next meeting was really interesting as each of the women talked. No ready solution was offered that could be implemented quickly. John had an idea and asked Marisol first: would she consider becoming Deputy Prime Minister and surrender leadership of the Parliament to Ellie? She was shocked.

Ellie was even more stunned as he turned to her and asked if she could and would lead the political debates if Marisol moved over. They would take another two days to consider these changes, but he asked for an answer by then. When they returned, he asked for their decisions; both were reluctant but acknowledged that support for the executive was necessary and so accepted. Ellie added one condition: she had an administration assistant, Philip

Jones, who had proved talented and eager and asked that he could try the Cabinet Secretary position on a trial basis. It was agreed between them all and so next day, details were given to the media. The changes were:

- Marisol Mugave – Deputy Prime Minister.

- Ellie Magellan – Speaker and Leader of the House.

- Phillip Jones – Cabinet Secretary and temporary head of the Civil Service department.

John next held a private consultation with the replicant officer who had volunteered comment through the medium of COMAS. Additional trained secretarial and office staff would be programmed to man the support teams. COMAS would co-ordinate the service and report directly to John.

John had done all he could to ease the course of the political establishment: time alone would validate his choices or not.

Chapter Twenty-Eight

The first Parliamentary session for the new executive arrived quite quickly and seemed orderly and not too fractious, at least at first.

Once again Eli Levine took the floor, reporting that the Treasury reserves were almost exhausted and all other business must be delayed until funds were available. However, he did have proposals to put before his colleagues: VAT levels would have to be raised from the current 10% to 15%.

Income and corporate taxes would have to be levied quite soon, but for two years would be delayed so that profits, income and wealth could be generated and hopefully accumulated.

Ellie had talked with Isaac Rosenblum in London about the issue of gilt-edged bonds for £25m repayable 2150 at 3% per annum interest. Rothschild's and HSBC Finance were prepared to underwrite such an issue for a reasonable fee, plus guaranteeing full take-up.

Interest at 3% per annum would need to be serviced from Treasury savings on Mars: say £750k per annum, which should be possible. Temporary loans might be available for any modest shortfall but would inevitably be more expensive.

General discussions continued for several days by video link and would be voted on at the next session. Everyone breathed a sigh of relief at the prospect of monies to be made available in due course, but there were reservations about the Colony being saddled with long-term debt and delays in raising taxes.

The next session proved lively as every Minister had suggestions to raise and points to be made. Soon John, Marisol and Ellie had to intervene to ensure each important question was discussed properly and dealt with before a vote was taken.

Ellie made a statement too; she as the Speaker would try to ensure every Minister had the chance to speak, but a hubbub could not be permitted.

"Some of you," she said, "are shouting and quite clearly not listening to the views of others. In future, you will all submit your questions and suggestions directly to the Cabinet Secretary. These will be collated and a brief available to everyone 24 hours before the next meeting.

"The open session will be directly under my control and once the person submitting the question starts, a general debate will ensue. However, to ensure that each Minister can be heard, questions from the floor may not be called out. You will raise your order papers and signal me – I will then offer you the chance to speak, to raise questions and make your contribution.

"My rules for this house will be published tomorrow, ladies and gentlemen. Robust debate is desirable, but we must not quarrel or squabble in public. Government is too serious for that."

The vote on the motion put forward by Eli Levine then went ahead, and of course achieved the majority necessary to proceed.

The local media did make quite a show of this session on TV and screen. Ellie Magellan was unknown to most of the Colonists, but she certainly had their support.

Chapter Twenty-Nine

Everyone in the Colony felt the pressure of these early sessions intensely; there was so much of their future resting upon the success of domestic political control.

John knew that until the Stock Market in London and New York reacted and supported the Wave Colony – or possibly failed to do so – nothing could go forward.

He decided to call a Wintertime Recess and delay the next Parliamentary Session until March, a full six months away. By then Market reaction to the Bond would be fully known. The funds available to Ellie and the Treasury would be in their hands and the individual Ministers could begin to submit their requests and budgeted proposals. Meeting sooner than this would be quite pointless.

During the long vacation he would fly to Earth and meet with Isaac Rosenblum and be 'on site' when the bonds were offered for sale in November.

Marisol, Ellie and Eli thought his appearances on TV and the internet might help confidence in the Colony's future.

Some of the Colonists asked to join him for a holiday on Earth, when the news broke. He agreed places to be allocated by open lottery.

Sui and Tilda were overjoyed at such a prospect and asked to accompany him; of course he agreed. Who could deny him such a break? He had intended to visit Falmouth anyway because his brother's health was poor and there was much to discuss – not least, the future of Simon's wife Una and her daughter.

Dealing with domestic matters was something of a relief after weeks of tension and as he settled back into village life, he realised that home and belonging brought much pleasure and comfort. Sui told him about the high demand for survival suits in the village. Some of the available supplies were quite old now and nowhere near as efficient as his own Maglev suit. John promised to add modern suits to the next trade agreement.

He was keen to find out why there was so much interest in the Rift Valley, so he called COMAS for an update. To his surprise he found himself talking to Indira Khan. The sludge pool at Webb Land looked good but time alone would tell if the slime would develop further. She and her team had therefore moved to a new site in the Marianas Rift. An area about five acres in spread had been found south of NY Village. Analysis showed that the composition of soil and residues here could become fertile if properly protected from cold and fed with water. She and her team were busy establishing protective barriers like those at Webb and news had leaked when the boys were taking a break in the village recreation centres.

"I would not mind seeing that Ravine Site for myself," said John. "You know you can do anything you wish, anytime. I would love to meet you there and explain in person."

The daily video conference sessions with Ministers were decreasing as each colleague became more comfortable, so John told his family that he would take a day off the following Tuesday.

Suited and booted, he arranged to meet Indira then loaded his sled and lifted off into the dawn. The site was quite like most other sites: bleak, steep in places and with limited light because of high cliffs rising everywhere except where it spilled into the Rift Valley itself.

Colours were muted at first, but as the distant Sun rose, light and colour increased revealing a small plain, surrounded by marbled multi-coloured rock. Stunningly beautiful indeed.

Indira landed, her long dark tresses bound back. She, just like the ravine, looked wonderful. It was a pleasure to listen to her talk in her lilted English and he invited her to join him for lunch. Darkness fell early on this confined space so they left for home and base quite quickly.

Back home everyone in the village hall was keen to learn what he had seen. He asked them all to be patient for a while until Indira considered there was something to see.

Sui and Tilda were keen to hear about his day and suggested they would like to meet Indira and her husband too. He took the hint and stopped talking about her.

John found his days were growing ever busier; his Ministers' actions seemed to be sensible but all wanted confirmation and support from him and the internet sessions were growing longer and more complex. He realised that he needed to set up his own support team so that if necessary he could delegate the task of preliminary vetting to them. Marisol agreed that if he intended to wander off and visit Earth, she would need a lot of technical support to function well as his Deputy. An older woman, she had also become rather concerned about the demands being made upon him and said so.

He had obviously chosen well in offering Marisol the post, and she was becoming very protective as a good aide always should do. She had also taken charge of the selection process for the forthcoming Earth visit, much to his satisfaction. Ellie had settled also and assisted well.

The renovated vessels Dianna and Melany were ready on time and had been fitted out with accommodation units for each travelling family. John, his wives and children had a grand suite entirely to themselves as befitted his new status.

Mars society wished them all well and they lifted off in a blaze of publicity.

Chapter Thirty

Sui and Tilda loved their new quarters and the opportunity to comfort and love him quietly for the first time in nearly a year. The children, used to being with Gemma and Liza, took to being with Daddy too as their just reward for being good. Emma Linn and Henry John kept him in their sights as much as they could and loved it when he let them follow him to the quarterdeck command centre. Henry swore he would fly himself as soon as ever possible.

When Earth and its Moon Colonies finally appeared on their screens, almost everyone on board repaired to the planetarium and the observation room. Sui and John smiled gently to each other as memories of their first meetings flooded back. The voyage from Mars had been swift – eight weeks only – and everyone now started to pack for disembarkation.

There was absolutely no way to avoid a grand arrival this time. All the Earth and Satellite Cities had been bombarded with news for months. In addition hundreds of jubilant grandparents, siblings and other relatives were at the landing site, everyone making the most of this historic occasion.

Feted, hard-pressed and a bit weary, all the New Waves had to endure reception after reception before they could find some limited privacy and enjoy the holiday as they had planned.

John and his family were prime media targets, so he had to accept the offer of a bodyguard protection service provided by the US government. Free of charge, of course! The pace of demand gradually declined to the point where John could start to visit places of interest, though even there full privacy could not be achieved. The bodyguard service stayed and kept it all civilised.

John heard from Simon at his old home in Falmouth and arrangements were made for the farms and parklands to be made secure. The bodyguards were given special permission to continue to serve on English soil and several farm cottages were set aside to accommodate them.

Simon, Una and their daughter Louise gave the family a warm reception but allowed John to show his wives around himself, recounting stories of his early years and his parents. The children were enchanted, loving the house, the woods and the farm animals.

The tenant farmers welcomed all happily, and presents of food, wine and local delicacies piled up at the old Hall Manor. It felt just like Narnia to the children – and to be truthful John, Sui and Tilda felt the same. These family lands were beautiful and luscious compared with Mars. Even the weather made a special effort, clear and bright with gentle balmy seas kissed by winds rolling swiftly in from the south-west.

Emma and Henry asked to go sailing too, for some of the local lads had been telling tales about mucking about in boats and sailing along the coast. One or two of the bodyguard unit had sailed themselves as young people and offered to hire a yacht and take the kids out for a few days. Gratefully John agreed, although his wives were nervous and jittery until they all arrived back safely. The children had never seen a river, let alone the vast blue stretches of sea, and could not wait to sail again.

This shore-leave period of over a month passed all too soon and it was time for John to pack for the return to London for the Bond launch. This went well, so it was time to leave. There were many tearful farewells, for the children in particular had been loved especially by Una and Louise. John promised they would all return one day and left feeling quite emotional.

Chapter Thirty-One

Departing Earth with many a fanfare, John was not surprised to see that some families had not taken places for the return journey. COMAS reported that five family units had withdrawn officially and two people had just disappeared without notice. In their place sixteen young people had accepted the offer to join them. John met them all quickly and settled them into their own accommodation.

The journey back took a bit more time than the Earthbound voyage and the mood on board was much subdued. John was at his desk and working at the computer link almost every day. No change there, then!

But something had changed: despite careful health controls and personal monitoring by the COMAS servers, one or two of the passengers had developed symptoms of the common cold. Both families concerned were now isolating in the care wards, but it seemed the little beast had migrated and several more families were infected. Mass vaccination would be carried out now and no one, not even John, would be permitted to disembark on Mars until the carrier or carriers had been identified and cured as far as possible.

The dry cold desert atmosphere of the colony biomes must not be contaminated; Marisol reported that the media was full of stories about bacterial and viral infections. Dianna and Melany would be held in orbit until all trace had been eradicated, probably two to four weeks. John agreed – inconvenient but necessary – and news of the delay was broadcast throughout the ships immediately.

This first holiday outing to Earth would now end on a downbeat note; arrival back home would not be greeted with a fanfare but with suspicion. A great pity and a note of caution for all.

Talking these problems over with Sui and Tilda, they confirmed that many of their friends among the donnas were tearful too. So, after giving it some thought, he made a direct contact with Cho En Mai and asked him to prepare a series of programmes to explore the nature of the human condition and especially the fact that most bodies rely on bacteria and benign viruses to function properly and give us life worth living day on day. Obviously, some mutations in the performance of such aids might work to our disadvantage, until our immune systems learned to offset and cope with changes. Everything strives to live. Otto was asked to promote these new programmes.

The media commented that such dedicated education programmes were designed to calm fears and prepare for John's arrival home. They were quite correct. He asked the Health Minister, Elsa Van Dalen, to arrange vaccination against influenza for all vulnerable groups and to send knowledgeable staff or replicants up to Dianna to carry it out.

Several weeks later, quarantine was lifted and the travellers were able to go home at last. Marisol arranged to meet John the very next day so she could brief him on events occurring during his absence. The following week he called the Ministers to attend him in person and meet at the auditorium.

Each Minister was asked to report the present status of his department and explain any problems or difficulties experienced. One or two tended to 'grandstand' but John allowed them to continue. He assessed the reaction of other Ministers to such attempts and found much to interest him. COMAS and her servers reported on these reactions in great detail: many had been mixed and showed a lot of tensions, deliberately contained and controlled.

When the population increased, so would the stress of these Cabinet Members. The numbers of children born was still on the rise but the first truly Mars-born generation were already here, just like his own family and growing. On return to his home village, he and his wives noticed how subdued almost everyone was. After discussions with Sui and Tilda he spoke to the donna representatives in a formal talk, suggesting that mid-summer, now four weeks away, should be celebrated with a village barn dance and festival.

This old earthside custom gave everyone a chance to sing to country music, dance and stamp the floor for a whole evening. He offered to finance a big meal, such as a hog roast, ice cream and fruits and a soda fountain for the kids.

The donnas were enthusiastic, contacted several dance bands and engaged two singers and callers to operate in tandem. The main Congregation room at the Ark would be dressed brightly and with much greenery as possible. Tables and chairs would line the walls for easy seating between dances and to serve as dining places. Their enthusiasm was contagious and the general mood lightened. Thanks be to the gods.

COMAS and her servers were once again made aware of the mercurial nature of humankind.

On the day of the dance, lively conversations and some bad behaviour was quickly smoothed over as evening approached, by putting the children down for an afternoon rest.

The dance was a great success, especially with the children who had raided the sweet trolleys as often as possible while mum was dancing. The Village Elders, really quite young despite their title, decided that such functions should become a regular feature of their programme. The news reached the other Villages too and soon enough all had followed this lead.

Chapter Thirty-Two

Sui and Tilda announced that they were both pregnant again, probably because they had spent so much time with John in the last few months. They were now getting into their late thirties and laughingly suggested he take some younger lovelies to his bed. They made very sure he knew that this was just a joke, not an invitation to wander. He pretended he misunderstood for a few hours at least.

Contact with each of the Ministers was made several times a week, but all seemed well, each one making a real effort to contribute to the welfare of the people relying upon their services. The only real point of pressure was in the schools. Learning online was effective, but the young children needed a positive human lead and constant attention to deliver well. Older students who had shown academic learnings and promise would be encouraged to take on this task. John instructed the Treasury to fund this project immediately. Teaching was seen as vital throughout life.

With every day the population was getting more adventurous as families found they could be safe outside the biomes at least for a few hours, provided they adjusted their survival suits properly. Some, especially the unattached, found the newly flooded pool in the Rift Valley a real attraction, and soon some liked to skate too.

John decided he could take a few days break himself as long as kept in radio contact, and took his trusty Maglev sled off to the southern pole. COMAS tracked him all the time of course and he reported to his wives every other day. Fifty-plus and still active, they often bragged to each other.

A few days in the wild soon restored his good humour; the strain of leading was taking its toll, but it was clear that he must plan the finish of his term of office because as yet there was no man or woman ready to take over the lead. His own desires and wishes he set aside for now and returned to his family.

He did turn aside for a brief visit to see Indira and her team, still working and recording data in the Rift. The sight of this beautiful older woman soothed him as always and with pleasure he stopped to eat and talk. Rahul, lucky man, shared food and talk as Indira and the team sat about. Progress was slow but the Webb land site was developing. Sea-like grasses had taken root in this protected pond and the first plantations of lichen had covered a few rocks. Oxygen was being generated but as yet in almost undetectable quantities. The biggest success was the drawing up of water from the lagoon, which even when frozen in the night could create a sense of wonder and magic under the star-filled skies. John and Rahul started to speculate about the way ahead with the Rift Valley. With strong robotic mechanical support and careful planning, this deep valley could become a centre of human life, with even a reasonable degree of freedom. It was something to think about, plan for and hope to bring to a successful conclusion.

Life drifted on and the years seemed to have passed almost unnoticed. Two more children arrived: Jennifer Linn and Alice Mae. These girls were again so alike that many in the village thought they were twins. The two girls grew very close and were actually more alike in attitude than Tilda and Sui's other twinned pairs.

Both of John's wives decided that they had made a decent contribution to the population of the new Colony and in future would control their hormones effectively, so no more children. Besides Sui had at last qualified as a doctor and could use her skills in the maternity unit exclusively. Tilda had made progress too and now controlled her own high-rise horticulture unit, with much development work ahead. Plant protein of all types was much in demand.

She was trying experiments in tree growth too, using larch, birch and willow. The gravitation fields might need to be reinforced, but sufficient power was readily available through local wind and solar generators.

Vegetarianism was all for many of these young people, and the plants necessary to produce some of the more refined products had been brought in seed or bare-root plant form.

John often accompanied Tilda as she worked among the special plantations. Projects like the Dubai greenhouses and the Eden Project had shown that it was possible to grow temperate and warm climate trees under cover, so the biomes dedicated to producing a wide variety of fruits, nuts seeds and roots had proliferated.

Specialist producers had brought equipment and their own expertise to the new Colony, with the result that now mini factory units occupied space in each biome and made foods, vegetable dishes and milk for the Wave Villages.

Animals – for quite a substantial minority still wanted cow's milk, goat's milk and sheep products – were much harder to bring, but sturdy first progeny had been developed, protected and cared for during the long initial voyage to Mars.

Once landed and placed in special farm-like biomes, they had thrived. New bloodlines were introduced via artificial insemination and the number of animals under the care of herdsmen and shepherdesses expanded.

Naturally under such enclosed conditions, there was risk of an outbreak of swine flu or – for chickens, geese and ducks – bird flu. So, regularly, individual animals had to be culled and burnt, though they were composted to produce minerals.

These all called for the attention of veterinary surgeons and care assistants. Teachers and agricultural scientists like Tilda found the demand for their services was growing greatly.

The use of animals and birds enriched the diet of many and most used eggs daily. It also meant that slaughter-houses separated from the farms be developed. These were not popular places but being essential were often set some way outside the Village complex.

Elsa Van Doren suggested that one large slaughter-house should be contracted and all the nine Villages community should pool their efforts, hopefully making proliferation of such facilities unnecessary. This idea was very popular with the Executive and was adopted immediately. Special interest groups demanding food prepared in their preferred way could still be catered for; she particularly had in mind Kosher and Halal meats.

The other big problem concerning Ministers was the handling of waste, which was accumulating. They decided to follow Elsa's idea again and set up one large reduction waste management facility. Pollution of the pristine Mars atmosphere must not occur, so a large part of Treasury funds was set aside to purchase the latest *quick-freeze-no-waste* recovery equipment from Earth, which left only ash.

Funds were quite scarce and reserves limited, but in the end, Eli agreed to support the idea. The programme was appointed unanimously, despite the cost. Eli insisted they must now start to levy taxes; unpopular, but income must be found.

Chapter Thirty-Three

By the time of John's finished term, the terraform programme had made a very decent start but a host of difficulties lay ahead The earthside-designed programme had allowed for some problems and suggested alternative ways in which these could be dealt with. In practice many of these remedies proved completely unworkable, but with experience the Khans' adaptions could work reasonably efficiently. The questions arising might mean that the programme be further delayed while a solution was found.

The First Wave settlers had begun to get used to their quiet, easy way of life. Most of the physical work was carried out by robot and replicant servants and their need for food and entertainment was provided freely.

As a consequence, many folk were becoming overweight, over-indulgent and their physical condition was deteriorating. The number of newly born children had dropped.

The executive called in a team from the Medical Centre to discuss possible solutions; weight problems had at one time been a real problem on Earth, and had strained health systems resources. The solution had been to invite dietary control, increase the use of plant foods and promote fitness programmes. These alternatives were discussed at length and amongst others, Tilda was called to talk about diet. Vegetarianism was in fact widely practised within the Colony.

Some Treasury help could be made available but there were very few professional trainers, so initiative was needed here. One older practitioner, Simon Gusman, suggested a local version of the

Olympic Games might encourage participation, and this was also adopted.

COMAS was asked to find and televise the last series shown on Earth, so this she did. The Beijing opening ceremony with all its razzamatazz, music and marching athletes was broadcast that evening. The immediate response was disappointing, but day after day the events unfolded... and then followed the presentation of winners as their nations' anthems sounded in victory. Stunned at first, the daily audience grew and when the games ended in a haze of glory; almost all watched, basking in the music of their Earth home nations.

Fitness programmes became over-subscribed, individual and group trainers in constant demand. Sprain and other injuries were common and new physio services established. Running tracks and gymnasiums were in constant use.

Health and wellbeing were improving, so a summer series of competitions was proposed and agreed. In order to mark the gratitude of the executive these games were named The Gusman Series. One woman called Rita Janet Keain and her companions became dance competitors and the Treasury set aside tax money to fund training. Rita's dance classes were popular: she was once again pregnant but she carried on.

Soon the Colony would need to expand its territory and this would become a necessity as the children of the First Wave grew to maturity. Maybe, if terra farming could not be accomplished within one lifetime, the geneticist and trainers would have to explore ideas for living on Mars as it was.

Humankind had, after all, adapted to live in many hostile environments on old Earth. The executive called all Ark leaders to attend a conference in the new Caldera arena to consider ways to bring about change. COMAS asked to identify, list and broadcast a whole series of Earth programmes on environmental living. She agreed to help and answer any questions arising from viewers. The conference would take place on July 20th, after the Gusman series ended.

Chapter Thirty-Four

The population level of able adults was still quite small, with only thirty thousand over the minimum age of sixteen years. Nonetheless, each Ark community felt able to field initial trial sports during April. Winners and representative athletes would form a small team to represent their village at the Gusman games.

The competitions would be running (5k, 10k, 15k), gymnastics, archery, long and high jump, tennis, squash, boxing and swimming. Team sports were included to encourage more widespread involvement. Football, netball, polo and hockey were popular. Enough prizes were on offer to encourage participation by both males and females.

Family groups could become engaged later if an autumn series was called or demanded by the village Elder.

The excitement began as a slow burn but gradually built to engage the majority in one form or another of sport. COMAS reported rising levels of fitness, so even at this early stage the policy was being considered a success.

The Fisher Family Village (Europa) was alight with purpose. Training days were attended by almost every person, glad to have something to work on: idleness had led to indolence and this in turn to quarrels, usually petty, and to active acts of dislike.

John and Sui were pleased and the two older children, Henry and Emily, pleaded to be allowed to join in the Junior Games. Each evening after school, they all watched the day's training programmes and talked of their favourites, before settling to the evening music practice session. Bedtime came to the youngsters all too soon but they loved their evening routine of story and lullaby and drifted to sleep happily. If they were disturbed in the night, John would be there to comfort and soothe them, while his wives rested.

Sui was enjoying this period; Tilda was often away attending some conference or exploring and testing some new gadget on offer. Sui spent time with her friends in the Village and then devoted evening hours to study – mostly medical studies. One day she might even become a surgeon! Not yet though: she was pregnant again and this time was believed to be carrying twins again.

Life rolled on easily for these village groups and one or two of the unattached decided to settle, marry and join them. As the April trials approached, they all rooted for their boy or girl, but it was a friendly kind of rivalry, at least at first.

The Village Training Games convened; the people to be chosen began to emerge as lead possibilities and therefore rivals. The men in particular displayed this tendency, while the women, or all but one, cheered and supported each other. The exception was Sandra Mason who could throw a javelin nearly as far as the best man. Anglo-African in origin, she demonstrated real power. Added to this, she was also fast over one hundred metres. She kept to herself a lot but watched future rivals from other villages continuously, clearly according to her proud father, intent on comparing their performance.

She was far and away outstanding in her trial period and no one disputed her right to run and throw in the Gusman Games.

Most of the menfolk were pretty evenly matched but some had one or two skills in which they achieved more success.

Sui was invited to join the selection of five senior men and five older women to make up the number to eleven; this to avoid any impasse. Unlike the others, Sui had not trained as an athlete but she was generally regarded as a good judge of character. The training programme ended and by 5th May a list of all those who would compete in the Gusman Games was published. Much rejoicing and quite a few disappointments: roll on June!

John returned from his latest mission in the midst of all this excited debate and was concerned that Sui had got herself involved.

She soon set him right; she had accepted the role and believed it to be one more indication of the regard she and John had been given.

His concern for Sui assuaged, he did wonder if the Fisher family were becoming rather vulnerable as a potential leading group. He wanted to keep his family safe and could not wait for the imminent arrival of twins.

In the event Sui delivered her two girls exactly on schedule and a full three weeks before the Gusman Games. They called the girls after Sui Linn's mother, the first Jennifer Linn and her sister Ann Linn, with the surname Fisher of course.

Perhaps because he had been absent during the early discussions, the Gusman Games did not interest John greatly, but like a dutiful dad, he watched the programmes with Henry and Emily. Sui had to be at these games with the girls for honour's sake and was given pride of place in the judges' enclosure, although she would not vote herself, except to break a deadlock.

The games were a great success: the opening ceremony took place in the Great Central Caldera at night. This whole area had been worked by robot engineering teams. There were stands in the National Colours of Earth as adopted by each of the Village Communities, music, dancing and a parade of fabled animals mostly base on Mardi Gras characters in animalistic form. Flags and the athletes marched behind a replicant band in alphabetical order. The Chinese Government had shipped in a special array of fireworks for this sporting event and televised the whole programme back to earth.

Once this ceremony ended, all too quickly according to most people, the games themselves proceeded. The actual tournaments were held every night for seven evenings.

Prizes and medals were given as each contest concluded. It was quite a heady mix for the New Wave families to view, review and to love. The Colony was growing up.

The winners of medals became instant celebrities and were praised, harassed and adored, treated as heroes and heroines all.

In Europa Village, Sandra Mason had met and exceeded all expectations. She now held the Mars record for the javelin, shot put and the one hundred yards sprint. All her times were better than Earth athletes, even that of some men. She gradually relaxed a little in the afterglow of success and soon enough found herself a boyfriend. An athlete, of course!

The executive were pleased with all the positive outcomes and decide to opt for the Earth-style Olympic four-year period. The Mars games would be held out of phase with the Olympics, so Mars TV could give a proper weight to the smaller games locally. The Caldera was placed under the control of a permanent ground staff and would be used for unsponsored activity until needed again. A sports venue of their own.

Chapter Thirty-Five

These early years of consolidation were a blessing – most New Wave Colonists had dreamed about this future they had chosen deliberately and they were therefore generally in agreement about the way such a confined life could be lived.

The children, star-born on the original voyage or conceived on Mars, were of a different mould. Tough, generally well educated and – now John's term of office was drawing to a close – inclined to venture off in any way possible. They wanted to be considered and consulted about THEIR future! Many had been given opportunities to express their opinions and as they learned about the history of children's involvement in the politics of the twenty-first century, particularly in relation to the environment and climate change, they became increasingly aware of opportunities to develop personally. The main effect of this would be felt strongly in the future, so each child would be given the opportunity to study on Earth, hopefully then coming back home with lots of ideas that interested them and that they were keen to explore.

Many had ambitions – quite understandable for New Wave people – so competition for power and control would have to be carefully negotiated and perhaps moderated.

John decided to ask COMAS for a detailed assessment of this new generation and perhaps some guidance regarding the potential for real leadership. COMAS and her servers began the task of compilation immediately. They reported that there were some skills in the human arena that were rarer but which might enhance the chance of success in the next phase of development.

The deficiencies were rather primitive in nature but could offer instinctive advantages in the wild terrain of Mars. First was water divining; the records showed that all finds of polar frozen water had been made by one man of Aboriginal Australian origin. His children possessed similar skills and needed partners from the same background but none were available at present. Possible solution, an invitation to be extended to Aborigine communities on Earth?

Second, polar survival techniques based upon tribal experience in the Artic and Siberian areas would be useful. Such people were not found to be included within the Wave population at all. Invitation again?

John thought about these suggestions; folk with these skills were seldom amongst the higher academic achievers but they possessed instinctive skills of a higher order for survival.

He decided to make a request via NASA and the UN. The response of Earth media was muted but individuals were quite supportive of the idea once they had talked it through in their tribal enclaves. Three strong young men and six women agreed to join the Colony. Quietly these peoples were proud to have been asked.

Their arrival on Mars caused quite a stir but the welcome extended to them was generally warm. New blood was welcome.

Going around the Wave Village as it had now settled down, John could see many differences culled from the Earth origins of its peoples.

Many of the biomes especially those erected by the families as they grew larger had acquired a style of their own, often related to the main religions and or the styles of homeland architecture.

Some looked Gothic, Grecian or Islamic, Chinese and Japanese. Folk had added some decoration in minimal style, or even in places recreating Zen sand forms.

So these changes represented what? A longing for home and Earth, or simply recreation of a beloved past? Perhaps as a final gesture he should enhance the origins of his Colony. Yes, he thought – a museum, art gallery and a library in the best traditions of earthside benefactors.

He issued instructions through COMAS and the work was started, at his cost of course.

Chapter Thirty-Six

I may have given the impression inadvertently that life in the confined and enclosed community passed without arguments, disputes and outright violence, if so, please accept my apologies.

Humankind continued to behave exactly as on Earth. Families became clans, clans developed rules and ideas of their own and leadership was often disputed. Rivalries, jealousies and ambitions often soured liaisons too.

As the years rolled on the media reported one such row which had tragic consequences. A young college lecturer, Jan Malcovic, who taught philosophy, often talked of attitudes and more with his students, and called for discipline and control.

One day he returned home to find his wife in bed with a colleague. After the ensuing quarrel his wife left to join her new lover, leaving behind their two young daughters. Jan comforted his daughters and soon arranged a young girl to join them and take over their daily care. Her name was Minnie Mullen, a fully qualified nursemaid. They all settled into their new life reasonably quietly but Jan withdrew into himself more as each day passed.

One morning Minnie found his bed had not been slept in; she assumed that he had worked through the night and left home before she awoke. When he did not return at the end of the day, she called the Social Service people to ask for help in locating him. He had not attended college that day.

Investigators decided to ask Jan's wife and called at her new apartment. After forcing entry they found a grizzly scene. Jan had apparently come upon his wife and her lover in the bedroom. He had shot them both, then lying down beside his wife had shot himself. The bed and the room were awash with blood. Jan had left one brief note 'Death not dishonour'.

The Wave media was full of speculation but most folk understood: Jan had loved his wife but would not share her favours. A premeditated act, then.

The children were not told and lived on with Minnie, who soon married and gave them brothers and sisters to play with. She also inherited the home.

COMAS and her servers noted once again the vulnerability of humans and checked all psychological profiles. They did notice a fall in casual liaisons for a time, but memories are short and normal behaviour soon was restored.

Marisol called upon the Matriarchy asking if they had any idea how such behaviour could be avoided. They had no ready solutions: love, hate and jealousy were simply part of the humankind general behaviour patterns. Religion might help, they suggested.

One other event was recorded and made the subject of comment and eventually the establishment of a medical service to deal with psychological disorder and breakdown.

Most Colonists had adjusted reasonably well to living in confined and crowded accommodation, but a group had formed to rebel against parental and family control. Many were from Indian and Arab families which clung to earthside ideas and organised formal rules governing behaviour.

This younger element wanted to break with traditions especially those controlling the lives, education and attitudes of females. Some among the Colonists had never accepted the idea of matriarchal control and refused to conform to rules governing the role of men.

The case in question arose because a couple of sisters of Arab origin fell in love with Jewish lads that they had grown up alongside. All went on quietly and surreptitiously but when they reached puberty, they let it be known they would marry out of their faith.

The rows, fights and arguments caused great distress, and with the support of others in their group they planned to act together. Pressures mounted until all finally had been said and the sisters had been locked away in the family home. The boys equally determined, kept calling and eventually brought their complaints before the Village Elder.

While negotiations continued, the girls somehow broke out and met the lads and sledded to a distant oasis, causing general outrage and talk of vengeance. The search party found them together, masks off, lying in peace under the dark skies.

Within the Wave Village, services of mourning were held and bound almost all families united in sorrow.

The number of children expanded, so two more nursery schools were built and opened. Eventually one would be upgraded to provide classrooms for A Level study, up to age eighteen. Beyond this, an entirely new complex would rise to take them to university stage for those pursuing trades to the end of schooling years via apprenticeships.

The family homes were of course, growing too; each clan moved to the outer ring of biomes and from there constructed linked units in which to live and work. Single folk or those with one or two children only, tended to move to the inner ring around the Arks, where life was more communal and engaging. In this way the community was becoming more stratified and complex.

John and his wives had chosen the outer ring and as the years passed they followed the trend towards outward, V-shaped expansion. Sui and Tilda were especially proud of the latest unit which had solar room and a music room with wide-ranging views of the red desert – and the skies. They had their own private air lock system, with a storage unit nearby for sleds, tents and exercise paraphernalia. This entrance was used rather than the public road and path system if they were travelling away from the village.

Gradually the children began to range far and wide; in time they all left home to set up themselves independently, gathering for special occasions only.

Chapter Thirty-Seven

The atmosphere at the Fisher family home underwent a distinct change: only one bedroom was kept, because on occasion Henry John returned from his travels and until he married, he would expect to visit his home.

The Tilda twins decided to stay together and moved to an inner ring apartment where within days the Sui twins joined them, all young girls together, still studying; they were keen to party in their free time and could all monitor – even steal – each other's boyfriends.

William moved on to a splendid new apartment where he could maintain a decent standard of hospitality in his bachelor pad. A lot of the money received from John was used to support these ambitions. Unattached girls loved it especially the music and lighting system, which could be dimmed by voice control. The lights were regularly turned down or out.

The other girls and boys also left to live in the inner ring, nearby to the twins, but not too close for comfort. Edward Leesunn Fisher took up residence with Rahul and Indira to gain experience and to work at the Rift, as fun began to pall. No one had any doubts about his eventual success.

For a while the solar room felt empty, but Tilda and Sui brought in a small swimming pool and sauna. Within days their friends were filling the empty spaces. Extra staff were employed to keep everyone happy. John spent more time in his study or travelling around unless needed as a host.

Chapter Thirty-Eight

The Colony had fulfilled the wishes of the founders and was now a truly matriarchal society, with female leaders in most Ministerial positions and in this they were strongly supported by the Madonna Institute.

The newer satellite colonies were patriarchal and some frictions arose from this difference in control structures, but John and his team had been able to counteract adverse effects, mainly because of his personal status.

Now as his fifteen-year tenure of office as Prime Minister was drawing to a close it would be important to retain some continuity. The decision to raise Marisol Mugave to deputy had resulted in strong leadership even when John was temporarily absent and he knew she had valued the friendship and support she had received from Ellie Magellan as Speaker.

He had originally thought terms of office should be limited to ten years maximum, but now believed that his timeframe had been too short and an element of continuity was desirable. With this in mind, he called Marisol and Ellie to a meeting and proposed that Marisol should become Prime Minister and her successor, Ellie, should take up the Deputy position.

They were both surprised. John's views on short-term control of Government positions were well known. They asked for three days in which to consider his offer: he agreed, naturally. He also said that the younger generation, although talented, needed a little more time to mature. In due time both women accepted their new roles.

It was certainly true that some of the upcoming generations were showing real talent. Rahul and Indira's children had been raised traditionally and had proved academically brilliant in all matters related to biology, archaeology and geophysics.

Another boy, Johnathan Yiang – a US/Japanese lad – was a superb theoretical mathematician and quite outstanding computer scientist. He had already received offers from NASA, MIT and also from the leaders of Ausonia 1/Security Service. There was a likelihood that many others might be equally talented. So John asked for support from Marisol and Ellie in setting up a special support fund to ensure such people were identified and helped positively, despite possible accusations of elitism.

Education fees, lodging and support would be free to all regardless of financial status. Places at the foremost universities on Earth would be contacted as necessary. He asked Marisol to take the lead in presenting this special support fund to the next Ministerial meeting with his support, of course. This would give her start as PM a nice shiny beginning if agreed.

Marisol liked this idea and so did Ellie; one question was raised though. What if the candidate failed to complete their studies or even chose to withdraw? John said that punishment for failure should not be included in the manifesto. The idea was to promote the interests and opportunities available to all students. Punitive clauses would cause some less wealthy candidates to withdraw. The terms of the fund could be amended by popular vote of the public only, so no penalties.

All candidates should be notified of the offer three months ahead ,giving time for families and parents to be advised and invited to show their support. The plan was approved by the Executive, Marisol achieving a majority vote around 62% of those voting.

From this point Marisol took over and controlled most political discussions as John wound up his affairs and planned his retirement.

On his official retirement day ,the media and Earth TV services gave him a warm departing celebration. The screens were full of commentaries and pictures taken during his lifetime of service, together with a brief profile about his successes.

Chapter Thirty-Nine

The transfer of power to Marisol went smoothly enough until the election of new Ministers was announced. All those who had taken office under John and had earned support for a second time were due to retire. New candidates were being sought to replace them and the more ambitious in the New Wave Villages began to prepare to contest for the posts becoming vacant. Treasury, Education and Media were all coveted positions. Those Villages whose representatives had filled these posts felt it was their right to offer a replacement. Other villagers denied that succession was automatic and wanted to offer their own representatives as candidates too. It was time for Marisol to wield the powers she had inherited, but she would proceed with caution and consult widely before drawing up the list of those selected to serve.

Argument and debate raged throughout the Colony as relative merits were discussed and supporters of one disputed with those of an opposing view. Behaviour deteriorated and both male and female egos were bruised.

Families took sides too and none more intensely than the Rosenblums and Ambignales, often resulting in fisticuffs and street brawls. Ellie and Marisol tried to calm the situation by nominating their own intended family candidates and in doing so reduced rivalry amongst siblings. All these candidates were instructed to behave and lend support to the family representative chosen.

Julia Rosenblum was piqued that Isaac, her first son, had his own plans and so she nominated his quiet brother David. He was a good lad, she said, and would do as he was told.

Maria Ambignales nominated Angelina – not the most positive and ambitious of all her children. Angelina accepted and soon recruited all her siblings, boys and girls. Quietly talking together they could not understand why her very obvious drive and energy had been overlooked by Marisol so far.

There was plenty of competition from other families but the general situation improved as the final selection of candidates was made known. The community drew breath and awaited nomination and election dates. COMAS reported on all this turmoil daily to Marisol and drew up a shortlist of potential candidates for her too. Time to nominate was upon her so she chose one of the best from each ARK to face election.

Voting day was set for midsummer solstice and only those raising the most voters' support would be invited to join her team. Election drew the interest of media and even some comments from earthside reporters. On the day, three candidates triumphed:

David Rosenblum;

Arla Johnson, quite unknown to Marisol;

Roberto Mellison, a popular athlete of immensely powerful build and husband of Sandra Mason.

After interviewing each prospective colleague she offered Treasury to David, Education to Arla, and Roberto a powerful presence: Media and Arts.

Time alone would prove her wisdom or otherwise. She was glad, though, to note that Angelina Ambignales was not a voters' choice. She found her too contrary and quarrelsome. The candidates – now Colony Officials – took over their respective departments and set to work.

The disruption to daily life caused by this uncertain system had bothered her. She asked Arla to set up a special course covering power politics, economics and history, and decided only students who obtained honours in these subjects would be shown preferment in future elections. College Curricula would be annotated to this effect. Others might try for office but would have to show exceptional promise to succeed. Formal barriers would only cause tension.

The remaining posts would be filled by candidates who were particularly popular, but with records showing some talent or appropriate skill. Marisol chose carefully, mostly from candidates with strong support at home base.

For Science ministers she appointed Sandola Khan, one of the daughters of Indira and Rahul. She would be strongly supported by all her family.

For Business and Economics she decided she must ignore her personal dislikes and appoint Angelina Ambignales, reasoning 'let's see if she really is as talented as her family believe'. She also soon realised that this appointment had pleased David Rosenblum; he would work quite closely with the young woman over the next five years so it was good that they were friends.

As for Politics, just like John she decided this post would be her sphere of direct influence. Her Deputy, Ellie Magellan, would have many opportunities to show initiative too, perhaps more duties in due course.

One surprise during this period was the declaration by the younger Mars-born that they intended to create their own political party. This they would call the 'New Wave Democrats' and they intended to contest all appointments in future. It was time for the Earth-born to move over and leave Government to the young.

Rather defiantly, they raised a new flag; red, of course, with a central circle and a black figure 4, intended to mark their respect for the four dead lovers. This move created the first and only Martian Political Union so far.

Chapter Forty

For her first executive Cabinet Meeting as Prime Minister, Marisol chose to raise the question of relationships with Ausonia 1 and Maharastra, seeking the ideas of her new minister and colleagues. They suggested it might be useful to set up diplomatic services. Earth people had done this for generations. She considered this seriously and then asked if any could name and recommend a psychiatrist or diplomat skilled enough to undertake such a role. Only one name came to mind: John himself, but she decided not to make such an approach as John deserved a break. Instead she set COMAS the task of trawling through the class records and achievements seeking only young persons showing possible talent and old enough to join her team, a difficult task.

There was no one available at this stage in the Colony file, so she would add this extra burden to her own list of concerns. This deficit must be addressed before her term of office ended, so she drew the attention of Arla Johnson and suggested another course: Civil Service Affairs and the Uses of Diplomacy be organised, perhaps bringing a lecturer/ teacher from Earth to organise it.

Her first period in this new role had proved interesting but very challenging. It was one thing to deputise for an absent superior and quite lot more challenging to actually become the final arbiter oneself. She hoped her partner and husband Enrique Mugave would be sympathetic and supportive. She decided to bring in extra support, a lovely replicant – one of the latest produced. Enrique could be quite sexually demanding and such a maid would help ease any tension arising.

Looking back, she could see that her husband had been left behind and neglected. Enrique had followed the usual course and taken three other wives, each of whom had borne him children. He would hardly notice any change. Perhaps, she thought, it was time for her to make other arrangements herself?

She had, after all, been working long hours steadily for over fifteen years as Deputy Prime Minister. She had paid scant attention to love and domestic bliss. Heigh ho! This is what happens when life is dedicated to work and ambition. Did she have any friends? No – maybe John, but then this was a working relationship only, not a bulwark against the world.

"Buck up, girl," she told herself, "you have a job to do yet."

She had, but there was no doubt that the amount of work and the number of urgent demands on her time were reducing as Ellie took on more and more responsibility.

Time to think then, and really begin to look at life ahead. Whether it was her age, now 44, her reaction to the Malcovic tragedy or simply the prospect of challenges, she began to feel restless and unsettled.

One of her last engagements was to open a brand-new nursery complex at the hospital. Passing through the general wards, she noticed the many young people either working on the wards or in the beds as patients.

Close to the maternity units, there were lovely young women, glowing with health and holding babies close as they suckled and fed. She felt sad – where were her kids? She had always wanted children. She took her time once the opening ceremony was done, to move along the wards talking to people as she went.

The next couple of days passed in a daze and alone in her apartment, she took a good look at her own body in her bedroom mirror. Slackness here and there, mostly around the upper arms and a bit of a double chin that spoiled the line of he cheeks and neck, but not too bad. Hair coarse, a bit wild and frizzy but dull dark brown and lots of grey. She had not really looked at her belly and vaginal area in years. Ageing then, but not too bad yet. A bit of attention here and there and a period of exercise should result in a big improvement. Yoga? Perhaps!

So ,what was she thinking of? Sex, a husband, a lover? No, what she wanted was a baby, children of her own. Yes, she wanted kids, someone to love and care for, someone for whom she herself would be special. A man? No, definitely not a man? Artificial insemination then? Yes, that would leave her free to take all decisions for herself. She would set up a meeting with her doctor for assessment.

In view of her present status all this must be kept private. She decided to talk to talk with Sui, not a friend but known to her.

Marisol called the hospital herself, not wishing to explain her purpose to a secretary. Sui was quite helpful but suggested they meet over lunch somewhere away from the media hangouts.

One week later, Sui called and set up lunch at the Star of Bombay restaurant. They both liked Indian cuisine, especially vegetarian dishes. Marisol arrived and found Sui waiting in a small cubicle dining area away from the windows.

Their discussions carried on through the lunch and for at least two hours afterwards. Marisol explained her purpose in detail and Sui promised to help discreetly, but first she suggested a medical check-up to assess her condition and a talk with a senior gynecologist and then consideration of a detailed report on the likelihood of success, before she decided to proceed. Marisol insisted she cover the costs; she had assets and reserves that had accumulated for many years. They parted as friends.

Over the next months, the assessment went ahead until Marisol called a halt. She must now complete her first term of office properly and take time to hand over efficiently.

The day arrived ("at last!", she thought privately) and put on her most brilliant manner, bright, assured and most of all respect-worthy for her final performances.

She had decided five years was enough and her Deputy, Ellie, would – she knew – be interested in succeeding her.

Ellie had been training for the task of leading the Colony, but Marisol had elected to retire far sooner than she expected. Together she and COMAS got everything sorted and a review of all the tasks falling to the First Minister was placed on her laptop, together with detail of the way John and Marisol overcame some problems.

At the next executive meeting Marisol notified her colleagues of her intentions. There was a lot of reaction, but a few were quite glad about a reshuffle that might open opportunities. Ellie took the decision to announce her own bid, hardly a surprise to anyone, and asked for support.

Two days later the 'Whips' reported that she had the necessary level of support, so a motion was set before the next general parliamentary session. Ellie got her majority, and approved Arla Johnson as her Deputy.

Arla had planned to start a family with her current lover, Lawrence Anderson, and perhaps get married first. But in view of these changes she decided to wait a while. Ellie had been thinking along the same lines until her boyfriend Johnathan Williams had departed with a new lover. Perhaps later once I have settled in, she thought, but with whom? Wait and see – there was no other person in the game so far but plenty of men friends. Marisol's departure went ahead and without too much fuss; the media got over its initial dismay at her desertion – she had, after all, served for over twenty years.

When details of the changes in the ranks of the politicians were announced, many reacted with disappointment. Why had they, the public, not been involved in the selection of a new First Minister? The commentators did not deny Ellie's efficiency but surely there ought to have been some consultation. The New Wave democrats insisted that their candidate, Athena Razzer, would have liked to compete.

Ellie and Arla coped with the challenge but had to explain that that the choice of First Minster was best left to the Ministers in power and the executive. Why, was the question? Reply! A leader cannot function or govern well without the support of these politicians. However, both had to concede the point about the involvement of the electors.

In future all appointments would be notified to the electing people before selection. Reluctantly, Athena and her colleagues accepted that the reasons given were probably valid, but they had made their point and won a concession.

Chapter Forty-One

For Marisol a new life was about to start; quietly and discreetly the insemination programme began. The first attempt failed but the second seemed to proceed well and she began to hope.

At the follow-up scan the doctors confirmed that conception had taken place and under their advice she began a programme of fertile exercise and dietary control. She even started to look trim when she checked her mirror image.

Gradually, physical changes brought some but not too much morning sickness, which she had anticipated anyway, having listened to many tales from mothers. She also took full advantage of the pre-natal clinic services and made one or two friends with younger women there too.

The next scan showed that she was carrying twins, which was great news: she had been listening to some internet chatter about the likelihood of multiple births from insemination donation, and two children – both girls – should be OK.

In due time the twins were ready to emerge and she decided to use a birthing pool for the hospital delivery. The first daughter, Ellen, was exactly twelve minutes old when her sister Edith arrived. Marisol had survived well, just a couple of stitches to repair some tissue stress and damage.

Tired but elated, she settled back on her bed with a child on each arm. Her breasts filled and when the children were put to her the pre-milk flowed neatly. Relieved and proud, she settled back to receive the congratulations of her new friends. She did decided this one experience of giving birth was enough for her.

The local media carried the story of the birth of twins and many friends in the Executive sent cards. Ellie herself found time to visit the maternity ward and seemed quite interested in the twins, although Marisol did not expect this interest to last long.

Marisol asked how the transition to the new role had gone, but Ellie was quite dismissive. "No trouble at all," she said. One point Ellie did mention during their talk was about the role of Cultural Ambassador that Marisol had raised. She thought Marisol should now concentrate on her daughters and leave all attempts at inter-community relations to others.

John and Sui called as expected about a week after Marisol left hospital, and asked if she needed help at all. The hospital almoner had organised replicant nursemaid services and this had been useful. However, Marisol said she would really like a human woman to join her as a companion and eventually take on the role of nanny.

She had thought a lot about her future and decided she would like to go back to a period of study once the initial few years of family life had passed. She also wanted to be ready to work and study with her daughters as they grew. So not just a nanny but a tutor too, perhaps.

Sui was more likely to learn of someone able to help them than John, so she agreed to keep an eye open for a possible candidate. There were still some single women at large amongst the Wave Village community.

Chapter Forty-Two

Over the last few years since his retirement, John had spent much of his time promoting the interests of MARCO. Inter-community trade on Earth had produced good profits and so he had been instrumental in looking after several native traders and community producers amongst those people left earthside to ensure regular supplies to the satellite communities in the skies above.

The re-wilding of Earth had produced good results as nature once again restored health to the planet, but few of the rather cossetted people serving these satellite communities showed any willingness to return to labouring in the fields and farms on the surface. There were exceptions and some young folk did make an effort, often quite successfully.

Inter-planetary trade had eventually proved costly, with great profits rarely seen. Still, with his 40% stake in the company he had become truly rich.

He was doing very little at home on Mars and got quite tired of buying trinkets, jewellery and objects of art and was beginning to find consumption itself boring.

Eventually, to save his sanity and wellbeing, he decided to settle down permanently at home on Mars, live and love his wives and seek a new role in the Village. With thought and some quiet research he decided to sell his interests in MARCO, bank the proceeds and start to concentrate on Martian affairs.

John took his time, leaving approximately £65m on money market service via Coutts. His wealth continued to accumulate; enough he thought. If he was to safeguard the future of his children and grandchildren, this money needed to be invested properly.

First he set £10m aside for his two wives, this would be left on deposit in London and hopefully would continue to grow. With £5m each, Sui and Tilda should be able to live comfortably for the rest of their lives.

Next he called William and Alice, Edward and Sophie to join him to discuss options. Despite their different individual paths in life so far, they agreed to work together to promote the interests of the whole clan. So ,what line of business did they consider offered possible growth? They all had pet projects but nothing specific to offer that would make anything like the return achievable by simply leaving the inheritance with Coutts. In the end and rather frustrated, John decided to split some of the money between his children now. Each would decide how to proceed in their own way. He would keep £15m – £20m back for his own use.

It was only two months later that Rahul Khan notified the Wave Executive that a major deposit of lead ore and silver had been uncovered deep in the Rift Valley system. Ellie and her Deputy, Arla Johnson, asked John to attend the Executive Committee meeting to discuss this find. Treasury would be pleased to add silver to its reserves, but the lead would need to be found a market where it could be used profitably. A weighty matter indeed!

Chapter Forty-Three

John listened to the ensuing debate with great interest; perhaps in this gathering of talent someone would offer a suggestion which could prove useful and even profitable to the Colony. Suggestions and ideas about the uses of lead were mooted but none seemed practical or even doable given the present low levels of manufacturing existing within this community.

In the end John suggested that basic details about the find should be loaded onto the COMAS database and she should be asked to offer a fully detailed analysis of the situation using old earthside information and ideas as a guide.

Having made this suggestion, he left the meeting. The meeting apparently continued for several days, then they finally decided to follow his idea.

COMAS eventually prepared a brief outline: lead had been used by mankind since Greek and Roman times. It was a heavy, natural inorganic mineral, crystalline in structure, it was soft, ductile, and a durable material. It resisted corrosion, was a poor conductor of electricity and had been extensively used where sound, vibration reduction and protection from radiation was required. Main uses were in paint, lead piping, battery construction and in the making of crystal glass. A suggestion was made to add lead to the plastic panels as protection against radiation in the construction of biomes. These panels were presently imported and could help radiation protection over the Rift Valley if produced locally. Lead could be injurious to human life, so robotic miners should be used to excavate this material.

The executive gave this review serious consideration but realised that a mining and refinement process would have to be started from scratch and would require serious amount of finance to bring to production.

Questions arising were how extensive these deposits were on Mars, how much money would be required to bring success and which group could be expected to carry such a project forward?

Most agreed that the Khan family and IMARCO or a new Mars company like it would have to accept responsibility. The meeting adjourned and Ellie invited the Khan family and the Fishers to further talks. Mining these deposits should be suspended until these problems could be solved.

The meeting of interested parties took place six weeks later. The Wave Executive team felt they should have overall control of, say, 51% but needed the Khans to run the project. On the finance question they asked John if IMARCO would put up money if given shares in the mining company. Rahul and his family would be prepared to invest themselves and offered £1.5m for a 15% stake in the new venture and in doing so valued the whole project at £10m, which was quite modest. John or IMARCO would invest in the remaining 34% holding. Making a profit or even covering costs in the early stages of development was uncertain, so success was not guaranteed.

Once these proposals had been made and agreed in principle, John decided to fund the holding inside the family and called the children to a conference. Under his leadership they agreed to take shares in a new venture: Mars Mining Co Ltd. (MAMICO) registered in New York and London. The Wave Executive agreed and welcomed the investment.

The new joint venture was now established. Mining, smelting and refinement equipment was imported and installed. Extraction of the minerals began in earnest once the robot teams arrived.

Talking things over with the children, John mentioned his age and decreasing energy and stamina. They were quite unsympathetic! "You'll be pushing the world and us for years yet," they said. They were probably right: a new interest, a new project and a brand-new company to guide to success – some of his original drive would certainly be needed in order to protect the family interests and those of the New Colony.

John took his time and spent days locked in his study planning, at least in outline, how these early years of MAMICO might be used. He decided the actual market demand for the products of the mines would be very limited despite plans for OASIS centres and the Rift Valley enclosure.

The only solution must be to widen the market by introducing trade with the Satellite City communities at Ausonia 1 and Maharastra. So he must make initial contact soon and try to get permission for a trade mission team to pay them a visit.

Chapter Forty-Four

By traditional rules in China and on Earth, a visitor is treated royally and often, but will not be engaged in detailed discussions on every aspect of the deal on offer. Indications of goodwill are usually plentiful but a trader cannot expect to get anywhere near a decision-maker for several months and only then if the trade is a good prospect for them. Otherwise, you will be received politely until frustration finally causes a withdrawal.

In John's case, the Ausonia 1 traders were curious as to what his intentions were. A protracted visit so that he could assess their progress? A spying opportunity? If not, what did he have to sell they could possibly want? Much of the interrogation interview was conducted in order to answer such questions.

It was a surprise, therefore, to find that John had come to buy and not to sell but the decision-makers still wanted answers so that their trading stance would not be compromised.

John explained his reasons cogently and as patiently as he could. He and the Wave Colony would like to buy medicines, herbal remedies, teas and silks He knew most Ausonia 1 supplies were brought directly from the China mainland. They finally agreed to supply in exchange for silver, not currency, and drove what they considered a hard bargain.

In view of his success, John moved on and asked to purchase a new environmental habitation which he had recently seen on offer on his TV screens. This was another tent-like inflatable yurt that, when opened, operated itself to reach out a series of ribs, then to slide on environment solar panel covers that could provide enough power for heating and cooking for those using the tent. Lastly an inner wall, with airlock entrances to both skins, slid into place. This yurt would sleep ten.

The demonstrators had permitted John to try one and he had been impressed. The negotiators were much more reluctant about supplying these for the Colony, but they would donate one to John personally, as a gesture of goodwill, in due course – not now.

He thanked his hosts and future trading partners and asked when the first deliveries of medicines could be expected. The negotiator would organise extra supplies to be delivered to Mars but in view of the time and distance involved, would not make deliveries four months. In the event of a medical emergency, they would divert some of their own stock in order to help. John thanked his hosts and returned home.

Now he had to get really busy. All existing Community stores were held at the Village Ark Central under Starlight Navigation control. So first, he must arrange a shipment of silver ore from Earth, then start the trading missions in earnest. He and the Khans used their existing small staff at MAMICO and at the Rift to start two new ventures: first, a storage security for the silver, then a smelter and extrusion plant factory at the Rift. He would need robot workers and record-keepers at least. The Wave First Minister, the Government and Executive perhaps would require record-keeping by a bureau too. Some Treasury help would be useful for this purpose. They did, after all, have a major investment to protect.

The negotiations must begin now, so John asked permission to address the Colony Representatives as soon as possible. Ellie was agreeable.

A wave of excitement passed through the whole Colony: a serious business with lots of opportunity for personal development and growth. On the move at last, they said.

Rahul and his team were to be at the heart of the mining operation and would need extra robotic help. John sent messages to Earth: 'The next shipment must include at least one metric ton of silver ore and a dozen advanced robots with full mining capability.' All would be done, they responded.

Ellie co-operated too; a full boardroom session was set for the next Tuesday at 10 a.m., but she and her team wanted a full brief to be prepared and delivered a soon as possible before the meeting.

John, with help from his son Edward and COMAS, began working on the first draft immediately. Sui also offered comments on the storage, and viability and the uses of the Chinese medicines, together with a programme to cover future training for staff at the hospital. Sui suggested that a separate section team be enrolled perhaps with help from the Ausonia 1 Medical Sections. The hospital should see both humans and replicants train in the techniques.

John did the same thing for the mining operation, the establishment of a new warehouse, clerical support and estimated possible demands upon Treasury resources. Revenue flows were quite another issue and he suggested a formal approach to Isaac Rosenblum, now an influential figure in the City of London for support. David agreed to undertake such contact.

So far, the Mars Colony had relied implicitly upon the finance and support provided by the Earth Satellite cities. This could be a first move towards some independence. IMARCO had only filled a role as enabler; with luck the MAMICO could achieve similar status and results.

The news media were in a frenzy. "What's going on?", "Why were we, the people, not told?", "What is going to happen in the future and what are the implications for our health and welfare?" They were very good at posing obvious questions, but the main reason for such anxiety was probably that they had been ignored so far.

New ventures like these could never be trusted and even within the Colony everyone had to await the outcome. There was even more speculation in Ausonia 1 as the media there picked up and ran with the story.

Chapter Forty-Five

John was beginning to feel the strain himself: from standstill to 90mph in sixty seconds! He called in and briefed his children, even including the youngest. They would all be involved with these projects in due course. They crowded around him and the TV screen as he outlined a possible future and his ideas about where they as individuals might serve.

Later over drinks and snacks they all sat round in the solarium talking excitedly. John asked that they keep all his comments confidential.

That night and rather exhausted he talked quietly with his wives, bathed in the soft red glow of the night.

"I am now in my sixties," he said, "and I face the prospect of being closely involved in the development and success of these enterprises. I will not be able to spend a lot of time with you, my lovely girls. So, I have been thinking – you are both in your forties, vibrant and full of life. You have given me much pleasure over the years and a roomful of children. If you feel inclined to take a younger lover to help you bloom again, I will raise no objections, even if another child is born as a consequence."

Tilda answered first: "No!" she exclaimed. "I have thoroughly enjoyed being your wife and I have no wish to return to 'wild boy' lovers."

Sui was even more specific: "There was no one for me before you and I want no other. A one-man girl, and *you* are my man."

That night they all retired to bed together with the wives kissing and cuddling him from both sides: sheer bliss.

His first task next day was to talk with Rahul and Indira Khan and invite them to join him and Sui on the platform at the next parlay meeting. Questions about the extent of the new deposits of silver ore and mining were bound to be raised.

The meeting took place on the Tuesday exactly as scheduled in a blaze of publicity. All the media companies were there including several earthside news services. The ideas behind this Marside barter style of trading were explored in full because general co-operation between the Colonies had not happened before at leadership level.

Eventually, even the hardest opponents of the change could not raise any new points, so John asked the Executive to take a vote in order to judge the level of support for this initiative. The result was conclusive: 59% voted for and 15% voted against. The remainder abstained; the deal could go ahead. The second generation now had actual prospects ahead of a better life.

The following month the shuttle trading vessel arrived carrying the newly built robot mining team They took the sled immediately to the Rift mine site and were quickly set to work. The silver bullion consignment was larger than expected and thanks to Isaac Rosenblum, consisted of bars, all refined Sterling silver, valued at around £15m pounds. A massive boost to the Treasury funds, which was taken straight to the Colony vaults.

Ausonia 1 arranged delivery of the first consignment of medicines, herbal and rustic remedies and took home a payment in silver as agreed. The medicines were taken straight to the hospital and the panacea remedies to the street pharmacies and online traders.

Within days the Ausonia 1 carriers delivered the less important but more commercial teas, silks and cottons. The market traders in the central squares now attracted greater numbers of interested buyers and many new partnerships and outlets started up.

At last there were some things they could buy, sell and trade in with a prospect of real profit. Wealthy intermediaries stepped in to stockhold as fresh supplies arrived. The colonists noticed a growth in family enterprises as individuals began to establish fashion workshops and manufacturing to bring old skills back into use. Quality and fashionable demand increased exponentially.

Chapter Forty-Six

This flurry of activity and opportunity had not gone unnoticed in Maharastra Colony and the Community leaders contacted MAMICO expressing their interest in trade links.

India had traded with Western nations for centuries even before the arrival of the East India Company and the domination of the British Empire. Culturally were part of the Indo-European nations and many native skills employed in meeting demand for cotton goods, food stuffs, spices, and music. They could offer much and benefit their own people too.

John could see that the opportunities for business were extending. The three individual human colonies were taking advantage and interdependence would grow in time. Already he had seen Chinese and Indian business-people working in the market squares at Wave.

He called the family to a meeting to discuss the opportunities open to all his children. The MAMICO was really going to be engaged for some years on the Rift development project, so other chances for creating wealth might be missed.

He asked if any of them would be interested in running a new commercial enterprise to develop and meet such chances.

Emma Mae Freeborn, Tilda's first child, said no – she had always helped her mother and Sui with the other children and wanted to continue to work as a children's carer.

Henry John, the next born, had no interest in such business at all. He had, all his life, wanted to wander the skies; his early enrolment at the Skylight Navigation Centre had recently been completed and he expected to be offered a place on the next expedition to Jupiter.

Edward Lee liked the idea of development but was heavily involved in MAMICO at this time.

The twins – Sue and Sian Yenn, and Rose and Mae Linn – were very interested. They could combine the money inherited from John and set up a formal privately-owned trading company. Their individual skills would ensure diversity in the range of their interest and product ranges. A company – Yen Linn Co – would be set up now.

William, Alice, Sophie and Fisher John were interested but their personal development and achievements were all in the fields of engineering and science. They would all be happy to invest with the twins' new venture.

Jennifer, Ann and Fisher Alice Mae were both still working at completing their studies and would prefer to work on these, rather than pursue commercial interest at this time.

Time for all now to buckle down and get on with a living. John sat back; he would act as advisor if needed but would no longer take the lead.

Relieved, he decided to spend a few days cruising the wilderness on his own. Sui and Tilda agreed he should take a break because it had been quite hectic here for a while. In solitary splendour he set off the very next day, sledding along towards the Northern Pole in no hurry at all. At one point on the Northern Way he could see a line of camels carrying goods snaking away towards Maharastra but decided not to call upon them. He did, however, stop at one of the oasis sites some one hundred miles further on.

A small trading post had been established beside the water source and he had a fine meal of lamb curry before continuing on. He eventually reached a high plateau, pitched his tent and sat back to watch the night sky and his day ended. This night Deimos and Phobos were in the sky together... wonderful!

When John finally turned south to head home his eyes registered a glow rising in the area around the Rift Valley and was rather disturbed to see light pollution marring the night sky. He decided to visit the valley anyway on his travels and suggest the cessation of activity at night.

The development of the Valley was proceeding at a fair pace. Under the sky shield, several lagoon areas had been created and the shores all had lawns and sandy beach areas. Away from the water stands of trees, shrubs and some undergrowth was being established. Half of these pools had been turned into recreation areas for the population of residents and Wave Villagers.

The light pollution did not come from these facilities, but from the mining and factory area, which was still manned even at night.

John decided to stop, talk to Rahul, Indira and the research team to see if something could be done to mitigate the nuisance.

They all met next day for breakfast to hear what John had to say. Several of the miner teams were taken aback;, they had not realised the noise and light could cause a problem. The Rahul family was sympathetic and decided to use only replicant labour at night. These robots could use infra-red to work by, cutting flood- and search-lights wherever possible.

Chapter Forty-Seven

This year John would reach the age of eighty on 20th July. He wives wanted to make this day special and to invite all the family and friends.

Sui and Tilda booked the chosen venue and had thoughts to reserve a new lagoon park recently opened in the Rift Valley. They had organised several street cookshop chefs to prepare food, two orchestral bands to provide music and asked the twins' company, Yenn Linn, to furnish the pavilion and surrounding lawns with seating, tables and decorations and waiting staff. Food, wine and non-alcoholic beverages were to flow continuously throughout the day.

They next issued formal invitations to all they wished to attend including the Khan family. Most accepted.

The weather pattern in the days before had been chaotic, but then entered a period of calm. John's birthday dawned in a glorious if oblique sunshine and the temperature at the Rift site rose to a respectable 25 degrees.

By the time the first guests arrived they all decided to start the celebration with a swim in the lagoon. Youth and beauty was on display everywhere and great fun, even for the older women who sat around gazing at their children in satisfaction. Most of them were the Starborn, of course.

Emma had appointed herself hostess for the day and wandered from group to group with John, chatting, laughing and easing any likely difficulties. She even insisted John take a break to talk quietly with Rahul and Indira, who looked as beautiful as ever in a cornflower blue sari.

The main meal had been at 2:30 p.m., a really substantial and satisfying lunch extending to five courses, which took several hours to complete. Next, a few personal speeches, kept quite brief at the special request of John and his wives. Once this formality was over, all could retire to lounge about or rest until the evening partying began in earnest as dusk settled in.

Many guests stayed drinking and talking until the early hours of the morning, then went off to their own homes and beds. The younger unattached folk began to congregate, danced on into the small hours and as dawn was breaking wandered off to enjoy their time alone, mostly in pairs.

The media made much of the event and for some days could talk of little else. This grand celebration had also cemented the ties between the Fisher and Khan families. Edward and Shakira Khan would marry, and William and the younger daughter would make it a double wedding, all set for five months ahead.

Chapter Forty-Eight

The real surprise came one week after the celebration. David Rosenblum presented himself and very formally asked for permission to court Emma. No one was more surprised than Emma herself. She knew David, who had once been Chancellor and Treasury Minister, but had never considered him as a partner. As far as she was aware he was a mother's boy, and in any event had been in a relationship of sorts with Angelina Ambignales.

John was quite taken aback. Emma was the very image of her mother and had always been a guide and mentor to her siblings, but if Emma agreed to consider this offer, he would raise no objections. It was now up to Emma to accept or not. She asked David to meet her at a local restaurant in two days' time, when she would make her decision on whether to proceed.

Emma then set to work, talking with her friends, her siblings and people that worked around her. She learnt that Angelina had married Bolly Bolsonaro some years ago and like her mother had assumed control of family affairs. David's mother Julia had recently died of cancer and several friends speculated that was why he now sought a wife: he was very eligible, considered honest, was wealthy and connected.

When they met for dinner at the restaurant she asked David directly: "Why me?"

He answered: "I had no thought about marriage, even after the death of my mother and believed I would remain a solitary man. However, attending your father's celebration I was intrigued to see you, splendidly dressed and acting the charming hostess. The more I looked, the more I liked. You went from group to group, quietly, interested in conversation and making one or two really important points about your views of this new Colonial world we are creating, which reflected accurately my own opinions. I began to observe you more closely and could see you were sincere, honest and to cap it all were quite beautiful in your movements and ways of holding yourself. In short order I began to think of you as mine."

"What about your relationship with Angela?" Emma asked.

"Oh that," he said. "A lot of people thought we were a couple, but the truth is that that our friendship never did develop. I found her great to talk with, but she was too edgy and dominating. I had had enough of that from my mother. Now, let me make my intentions clear. I am the son of men who for generations had loved one and only one woman. If you will accept my courtship, you will find me patient, caring and only interested in our mutual pleasures. No outrageous demands or appetites, at least as far as I am aware. If you need time to think things through before giving me an answer, so be it."

Emma suggested they meet again in one week and thanked him for his consideration. One or two days later she sat down with Sui and Tilda to talk about this situation. They listened carefully but after learning about the way David had made his approach, could find no real fault. The decision must lie with her.

The next 'date' took place and this time Emma looked at him in earnest. He looked well dressed, handsome in a mature way with his short red beard, and intelligent. She decided to proceed and accept his courtship but make it clear this relationship would only give her time to make up her mind.

For a first real date, David asked Emma to visit London where she would meet his brother Isaac, his wife and family; she accepted.

They left by private shuttle two days later, leaving behind much speculation within the family. The wedding of the boys so soon upon them then took pride of place and caused a flurry of planning and activity. Rahul ,as the father of the brides, insisted on covering all costs. Almost unnoticed, Emma and David returned and moved in together: they had married in London by licence attended by Isaac, his wife and their children.

Although tired from travel, they felt it essential to attend the wedding ceremony and family feasting: spread over two days, it was tough.

Edward and William dressed formally in Western European styles, but the girls were in full Indian Wedding regalia and heavily laden with gold by all their relatives. Rahul and Indira looked good too, but the star turn among all the guests was definitely Emma and David Rosenblum.

She had had her hair re-styled short in a fashion like Mary Quant which complimented her simple but elegant lavender silk dress. High heels added to her presence. David wore a navy-blue tuxedo set with Cambridge blue shirt and tie. The strong colour way emphasised his reddish beard and hair. Quite a handsome pair indeed, as many remarked.

The twins and their friends gathered close around Emma, admiring her diamond engagement ring and the simple band. Emma was a bit embarrassed but did glow a little in all this attention. John, Sui and Tilda joined in offering congratulations but decided to leave questions to another day. This day should belong to the newly wed couples.

David had been cornered too but had fewer friends. So he just stepped back out of the limelight and watched until Emma could re-join him. They danced and then retreated to a quieter corner to be together and kiss. They went home as soon as they could, having done their duty.

About one week later, when all the excitement had died down, David arranged a formal dinner at the largest Village restaurant and after the meal pulled back a long curtain to reveal a storyboard five metres long. On it were photos, drawings and two maps. The first was of London, the second New York, marked to show the venues he and Emma had visited. He then asked Emma to address the family and tell how they had reached the decision to marry.

There were many questions, but everyone now could see and understand the changes which would impact on the happy couple. Simply, they were in love and love had changed everything.

Chapter Forty-Nine

Later that year John decided that his wives were right: he had helped sort life and business matters long enough. MAMICO and its business affairs must be handed to Edward, now acting CEO. John would discuss company affairs in future only if consulted.

The traders from Maharastra and Ausonia 1 were making real efforts to compete in intercommunity trade; they did not want MAMICO to be the only company trading.

Now the children were all becoming settled, John thought he and his wives should take a break and return to visit his brother and the family at Falmouth, before he got too old to travel. The youngest of those left behind: Fisher John, Jennifer, Ann and Alice Mae were all working hard at their education and could be left safely with Gemma and Emma on guard. They would clamour and express disappointment but he would make it known he intended to continue their education in England, probably lasting at least three to five years. They would be able to holiday at Falmouth then.

Sui and Tilda finally agreed and then began planning all the places they would visit during their stay. They also talked with Louise in Falmouth about a stay for a few days at least but Louise told them to come for a couple of weeks. Soon they embarked and used the long days of journeying to engage in keep-fit exercises and creating a detailed itinerary, which – of course – must include Paris. John sat quietly by, reading his latest set of papers from Oxbridge and MIT, which he had neglected over the last months. The reports from Earth environment agencies were making interesting reading and at last a secure future was in prospect.

The passenger vessel arrived at Canaveral Base with very little fuss, so the girls visited New York, while he took time to visit with some of his old colleagues. This involved lots of drink, good food and unending functions.

When Sui and Tilda got back, loaded with presents and goodies, they then packed these things into a small packing case for shipment on the next cargo vessel to Mars. Jon booked a private charter plane to take them all onto Falmouth, landing within yards of the old Hall to a rapturous family greeting.

Simon and Una were looking a bit tired but soon bucked up as they all moved back to the house and settled in before dinner. Louise, their lovely daughter, played host brilliantly. She had taken the primary caring role not just for her parents but half the tenant families as well.

Country life suited her well and as the de-facto Lady of the Manor had taken on all the duties of the estate. Her bailiff/steward – Armand St John – was also present at dinner; he had trained in France and Germany before moving here.

John noted Armand as he paid obvious court to Louise, but privately, Louise had made it quite clear she had no interest in marriage. She and her best friend Emily Manners from Silstead Manor near Truro were much more interested in the farms and their estates.

The family would probably have liked to talk all night but John and his wives were a little weary, so by 9 p.m. that first evening they all retired to bed.

Simon and John had a chance to talk more seriously the next day over breakfast. The ladies all decamped to visit Truro and would take lunch there with Emily at the Sun Inn, a place fabled for its fish dishes prepared by one of the top-flight chefs in the country.

The men were glad to drop the small talk. Simon wanted to explain the reasoning behind his withdrawal from direct involvement with the family estate and to discuss future ideas for future inheritance.

Simon and Una were reasonably healthy but were feeling their age: he was about twelve years older than John, his baby brother. Originally, they had hoped Louise might marry, have children and the problem of inheritance would be solved. But Louise was now post-menopausal and preferred a single life. Despite this, she had moped and acted quite unhappy when John and his family had returned to Mars. She had been loving the company of the young ones, especially when sailing along the coast.

Simon suggested one of John's children inherit the estate in due course. John liked this plan but would have to discuss it at length once back on Mars.

Later that night, dinner and conversation were both greatly enhanced when Emily came later to join them. It was clear the two women, now in their mid-fifties, were very close; just as well, thought John. Simon and Una were clearly tired and ate very little. When his hosts had retired, John called Louise aside to ask about their health and wellbeing. Louise made little of their ageing but from the way she had nursed and cossetted them it was clear she was actually very concerned and the main support in their old age.

Emily was even more direct on this subject: Louise was the main carer and the task of looking after both parents was a great strain, despite the presence of a nurse to help her.

Over the next week or so Louise and Emily took time to keep John happy and entertained, re-introducing him to all the tenant farmers and their families. His presence was very welcome and gave them both a break from routine.

When John mentioned his intention to visit London and New York, they decided to ask to join the party. Simon and Una had nurses and an extra maid could assist. She was permanent and had slept near to Simon and Una regularly. John agreed a little reluctantly, but reminded himself both women probably needed a break. They might also be useful as companions to Sui and Tilda, leaving him time to pursue his own agenda.

They stayed close to Covent Garden at the Cavendish, quite near the Strand and the Opera House. The hotel concierge advised John that a performance of Madame Butterfly by Puccini, was to be staged at the weekend, so he booked a box for them all.

The women went shopping and all came back with evening dresses that he was not allowed to see until the performance. Tea, wines and nibbles were soon organised for the interval and served at the box. Hang the cost!

Emily and Louise could talk of little else over the next few days, so leaving them and the wives to enjoy London, he made his promised visit to the Maglev Corporation at Cambridge Business Park. He was received with ceremony and given every chance to visit the factory and research centres. So many things were changing and new ideas were displayed everywhere. He left quite envious. He made a few purchases for despatch to Mars in due course, including a new-form Maglev sled.

Thinking of his brother and Una, he ordered and paid for a small six-person transporter to be delivered to the Falmouth estate. This was fully automatic but under the control of a robot server. Simon and Una and the two young women could travel to any location on demand and without stress, right from the doorstep of the Manor. Louise and Emily were both intrigued and excited by this.

Next, he took them all to Paris, booked a suite at the George V Hotel and left them free to roam. He often walked the streets and gardens alone, taking his time and listening to street musicians and buskers, many of whom were very skilled.

Chapter Fifty

Eventually, with Louise and Emily back safely in Falmouth, John flew on by direct flight to Mars. He was welcomed by all: the children held him in thrall for days, begging for stories of his travels, adventures and thoughts about Paris. He had recorded some scenes on his phone and these helped a lot.

The boys and the twins were amazed at some of the pictures taken at Cambridge, further enhancing their own ideas about science and the invention of equipment. His wives gently reminded him of his promise to take them all to earth sometime soon; the children needed to see the original home of mankind in all its glory.

"We want to sail too!" the children said.

"Soon," he said. "Quite soon," knowing that it would delight Louise.

Quietly over dinner one evening, he talked with Sui and Tilda about the future affairs of the old family lands at Falmouth. They were intrigued to think about such a prospect and agreed to support any decision he made on this subject.

Such a decision would be fraught with difficulty: disputes over inherited property can split and divide even the closest of families. John's own parents had faced such a problem. When his grandmother died at the age of 87 in her London home, the family could find no evidence that she had left a will. Disputes over ownership of the house and the thousands of pounds sterling discovered under her mattress had split the family apart. Two brothers, Dickon and Henry, fought over every note and it took the courts and a wise judge to separate their claims. They both died unreconciled, still bitter.

John decided the only way forward was to arrange a London solicitor to consult with Louise, discuss her ideas and any contingent conditions she might wish to impose, and then offer one or two suggestions for a legal solution. Once this review process had been completed, John would call all sixteen children together and place the proposals before them and await their comments.

Decision made, John spoke to the family solicitor, Gurney and Reece based in Truro, and asked them to handle these delicate discussions. He agreed to meet any costs himself, including reference to legal opinion in London. Will Gurney promised to research land and property law and take advice if necessary. John was glad for his help. Will knew all the affairs of the Falmouth estate and helped Simon quite recently. John felt quite relaxed knowing the problem of succession was in good hands. He turned his attention back to Mars.

About four months later, Will Gurney wrote a long letter accompanied by a short note from Louise. A number of possible alternatives had been considered by Simon, Una and herself. Enclosed were the details of the scheme they had preferred. She asked John to place the ideas before his family and to accept or reject the succession. No action would be taken until acceptance had been agreed.

The scheme placed before the family meeting read as follows:

- Full legal title to the Fisher Estate would be passed to a private limited liability company. Once incorporated, ownership would be reflected by shares.

- This company would issue 180 shares with a nominal value of £100 per share.

- Ten shares would be allocated to each of John Fisher's children, ten to Louise.

- Ten shares, called Founder's Shares, would be issued to Louise, as steward presently in charge. These Founder's Shares would enjoy special powers.

a. The right to call a General Meeting.

b. An absolute right of veto. In other words, no action could be approved without the steward's agreement.

c. Shares in this private closed company could not be traded on stock markets but could pass for value given to existing shareholders.

d. The position of steward would be salaried and the Founder's Shares would pass from steward to steward in future generations.

You can imagine how much discussion ensued but, in the end, all agreed the scheme was practical and would ensure that their rather nomadic lifestyles would have a firm foothold on Earth as a base for all family affairs. John wrote to Louise and Will accepting this plan. William and his new wife, Dana Khan, would travel to Earth in the autumn and begin studies in land management of estates. All were glad that the Fisher family connection for the last 350 years would be retained and looked forward to years of holidays in the Old Manor.

Louise, her friend Emily, Simon and Una breathed a sigh of relief and gave instructions to Will Gurney. After further discussion with his family, two places were booked at Otley College, Suffolk, to take the necessary courses starting in September. Land Management would be three years, followed by two years spent as part of a conversion course in Special Estate Duties. This would be a major commitment, so John bought a house on the neighbouring village green, so that William and Dana would be able to live together, work together and have time separate from the other course members. He also engaged a local builder to completely renovate and decorate the house. Once this work was complete, a housemaid, cook and gardener would be engaged and could settle into the house while awaiting the owners' arrival.

What a wonderful opportunity, thought William, but Dana had some reservations, not least leaving her parents, who were getting frailer as they grew older. Edward and Sophie did their best to reassure her, Earth, after all, was in constant daily communication with Mars and a Vid Link to Otley would be available for family talks.

Indira and Rahul could see Dana was concerned but after a tearful scene, managed to reassure her. They were still in good health and anyway had plans to revisit Earth, especially Pakistan and England, so would make time to visit William and Otley College.

John had made it clear the Khans were now family, twice-linked with the Fishers and would be welcome to stay at the Falmouth estate anytime.

Chapter Fifty-One

Months passed and life within the Wave Village settled once again into a steady rhythm. Tilda had her working hours and duties at the hydroponic farm, Sui was now a senior consultant at the medical centre. John had returned to his learned studies of intergalactic phenomena and in this received from COMAS updates regularly. He was extremely pleased that he had been allowed to retain these connections.

The children, especially the older ones, were getting ready to fly the nest and he took great interest in talking with them. The younger ones tended to look to him for stories about Earth and star travel, and still listened in awe.

Slowly, steadily, time had moved on and as each child reached adulthood they found more time for activities, swimming, climbing and prospecting – using the sled regularly. John did feel a bit-under used, so he called upon Ellie who was now coming to the end of her term.

Ellie had always worked diligently to try and bring the various communities now well established on Mars into a relatively cohesive whole, but in this she had failed.

The main problems were based on the fact that she was a woman, a mother and really had no opportunity to engage in business for a profit. She therefore had no experience, which meant that commercial jargon and laws relating to buying and selling meant little to her. Traders always experience difficulties if they are vulnerable, for others will note the opportunity to steal trade, pinch clients and exploit any vulnerability mercilessly,

Starting late and finishing her political career, she was simply ignored. The Ausonia 1 and Maharastra politicians simply left business activity to their traders. Formal contracts had proved unnecessary and often counterproductive.

Culturally, cross-fertilisation was already happening, Music, classical and based on the European composers of the last several hundred years, was regularly performed in the Satellite Cities. Their professionals took to making regular visits to the Wave Village to perform. African, Chinese and Latin American music was very popular, so folk rhythms, dance music and pipe bands were regularly seen in the Ark Halls and music venues.

In Ausonia 1 and Maharastra a great cult for Irish lilt and Celtic song cycles existed, so Wave performers responded willingly.

Ellie had already discussed the question of her departure and introduced John to her Deputy, Tamara En Lei, who would be expected to succeed her, although she did expect other candidates – especially Edward Bolsonaro – to compete for power.

Edward had socialist ideas and had already started to canvas the Ministers for the establishment of a parliament chamber. Tamara efficiently handled all crises and questions as openly and fairly as she could. Her influence among the leaders of the Madonna Institute was growing.

With her colleagues in the executive she was a little less forgiving. Loyalty and support she praised, dissention and opposition she punished. When her first secretary became pregnant and sick, she retired her and appointed the daughter of Amanda Fantini, a known feminist, to take her place. Tamara tolerated the male members of the inner cabinet but could not be influenced by them; her election was therefore uncertain.

The domestication of the Rift Valley was one of Tamara's favourite projects and she supported Rahul and Indira directly. Money from public funds was available and she made this ready for draw-down whenever needed. The Treasury Minister, Nicholas Callum, often disputed her priorities and was a source of friction.

Eventually her persistence did pay dividends; her name would be forever linked to Rift as a benefactor. Another major breakthrough came from her attendance at the Intercommunity

Council: quite overshadowed initially as the representative of a smaller community, she eventually became accepted as a champion of the rights of minorities and of women in Ausonia 1 and Maharastra in particular. These women still had to cope with dominated leadership so her outright support was both welcome and noticed throughout the cities.

By the time Ellie's term of office ended, she and Tamara were highly respected and awarded full honours. Edward was, however, elected PM.

Tamara retired and took up a teaching post at Wave and was eventually offered the position of Principal at the New Wave University, where she could still influence the young.

Eddie Bolsonaro would have to work hard to improve on her record.

COMAS was quietly amused: male or female, these human beings were so competitive. Good job the AI beings were generous and collaborative.

During private discussions at the Rift, Rahul left John in no doubt that the project had benefitted from Tamara's involvement. She and Ellie had regularly supported difficult projects. Edward looked good on paper but really did not have the knowledge, nor the experience, to assess viability. He and Indira now felt somewhat less pressured, which was good, for his sons and daughters had their own ideas and would take the lead roles now.

Edward Bolsonaro did in fact serve well and Parliament, long promised, was finally inaugurated. He had a quiet a but probing style and any speaker offering generalities or banal comment was soon confronted, often to their discomfort.

Chapter Fifty-Two

Within the inner cabinet Edward inclined to be conservative and willing to listen before offering his views. As far as the media were concerned, he was a bit too safe. No news about clashes or arguments in office leaked, so they began to turn their attention elsewhere.

The Speaker of the House position had been nominated and he, an intelligent Iranian called Armad Saudi Baghdadi, could always be portrayed and quoted as a powerful politician. Disappointingly, he generally supported Edward.

Towards the end of Edward's ten-year term the Wave community could see that the Executive and the Government had established firm but gentle control. The state was now truly benign, and an interested benefactor in times of trouble.

The true nature of Mars was still essentially hostile but co-operation across communities had established order, trade links and increasingly the ready exchange of ideas, music and culture. All third-generation Martian peoples would benefit.

The idea that politicians could actually work in a way that promoted goodwill and for the benefit of society was popular with the electors, but of course many would try and perhaps fail in the future.

Everyone old enough to vote began to look for a potential successor to Edward. Eventually the possibility of succession by a member of the Fisher/Khan family was speculated upon by the media.

Many of the younger members of these families received excellent education and several were considered exceptionally talented. Almost everyone agreed that they did seem quite patrician and not inclined to dominate community affairs. Others were less sanguine: harbouring ambition for their own, they fought each other to promote the claims of their own sons and daughters.

Such speculation was intrusive and the whole Fisher family felt such attention unwelcome, but it did cause much talk among themselves.

Edward eventually called upon Sui and Tilda to judge whether this media interest had been fabricated by them.

"No!" they said. 'We and the Khan family have made enough of an effort to guide and influence the future of the Wave Village community."

Edward departed: he was concerned about the future of the Executive and understood all his groundwork had produced a satisfactory parliamentary controlled democracy, but he was also aware that many did not share his social democrat visions. In addition, his present Deputy, Patrick Dempsey, did not wish to assume the First Minister post.

The presence of an intelligent but modest family who could be relied on to support the common interest was very comforting. He knew the Khans had a vested interest in the future success of the group. He decided to accept an offer of a meeting and to consider Alessa Khan as a candidate.

Discussion across the united family warmed up as each began to contemplate the implications of such a move. All the parents were troubled too and met to see if they could agree to a common approach and offer united support. They eventually agreed not to comment during the presentation but to insist their child must decide whether to enter politics and volunteer.

Overall there were many more females in this family than males and speculation raged throughout the next weeks.

The presentation of the case for entry was interesting, exciting in the way Edward saw future life. In this smallish world, they all listened with care as he made his appeal. Following a lead from Rahul, they told Edward their discussions would continue. In due course they would advise him of the decision, in good time before his term of office expired.

John and Rahul were undecided but caring. After all the bustle and battles of his premiership, Edward was gentle, non-combative and likeable. He also got to know Alessa, who had never before socialised. They liked to be together, so week by week he asked Rahul permission to court her.

Alessa was flattered but did she want involvement with such a politician? There had been some talk locally about a falling out between his brothers, Bolly and Angelina. Alessa had not been actively pursued by her friends and was often chided for lack of effort. She later accepted his offer and effectively gave up politics.

When the news broke on the media website there was a flurry of bitter comments. Here we are again, the Fisher/Khans building alliances again. Too much – too much influence, too much power.

The campaign for election began in earnest and played nicely alongside such comment, and when the election votes were counted, the New Wave Democrats had won power and entered Parliament. After their formal introduction many expressed their goodwill, despite their youth. Their current leader, Alicia Starborn, became PM and considered who to appoint as Deputy. It would be interesting to see how their careers in politics proceeds, not least whether they remain involved over the longer-term. Many would be happy to see them fail.

Alicia entered her office for the first time, carrying a rather bulky file which she slid into the secret drawer and locked after changing the code first. This would be her source book and fact file; it contained aims and objectives, culled from early speeches by John Fisher, with analysis and comment by her own father.

Chapter Fifty-Three

Of all John Fisher's children, my father Henry John was the most interesting and colourful.

Even while a student and before he actually joined the Skylight Navigation Institute he had a reputation as a philanderer, inclined to woo a girl, bed her then move on. Of course, this did not particularly endear him to many and he caused definite offence to one man – Pieter Van Damn.

Pieter, who had studied at Heidelberg University, had become a skilled swordsman, and when Henry stole away his favourite girlfriend, issued a challenge to a duel. Dad had never refused a challenge, so he accepted and they duelled at dawn on the campus ground.

He was swiftly defeated but not before Pieter had sliced a scar across his cheek, a ragged tear, like a big tick across his cheek, catching the bottom of his eyelid. It was a mark that dad carried openly and with some honour. In fact this gave him even more chances with the women, for a scarred man interested them and marked him out as different.

Later, after Navigation Training was over at NASA, he took flight and sailed the skies exactly as he had always intended. On one of these flights he met my mother, Lorna Carrington Jones. She was several years older than him but was petite and quite good looking. She had, he said, a way of looking quite demure but was also a very determined woman.

Something about her, and he could not say what, caught his eye. She refused his attentions time after time before finally the loneliness of a long flight in limited company inevitably brought them together. Henry was hooked; she became his lawful 'sea wife' and in due course I, William Henry ,was born.

Both my parents were far too nomadic to stay on Mars for long and by the time I was three years old I was passed to Aunt Emma together with my new sister Joyce Carrington Fisher, to be cared for. How lucky for us both! Emma was a lovely good-natured woman, highly intelligent and intimately linked with the children of John, Sui and Tilda Fisher. Consequently we were immediately part of a really closely connected family unit. David accepted us willingly.

We got to know both John Fisher and Rahul Khan well and always listened intently when family matters were discussed, including tales of my dad.

It will be apparent that I did not see much of my parents and about the time I was seven years old, news of their whereabouts ceased. I learned many years later that the Institute ship carrying them lost contact during a solar storm.

It affected me but in rather an indirect way. Studying space, deep space and the many multiverses through all my formative years, I eventually became a teacher and an author of some standing. I still wonder sometimes if that vessel is still tumbling through space above me.

Perhaps the greatest influence in my younger life apart from mum and Emma was my grandfather Rahul.

He was an upright, honest scientist dedicated to enabling mankind to adjust to life on Mars. He helped me to understand the difficulties that were being encountered and the rewards that would flow if these could be overcome. Even when really too young to take risks, he would let me spend a day or two with him in the wild. It was because of this close connection that Indira passed all his notebooks, drawings and idea lists, concepts and inventions on to me when Rahul died quietly in his bed. I was sixteen. This material and his old personal computer programs formed the base for all my own writings and many of the classroom lesson plans too. I kept in regular contact with all the Khan families, now close kin and regularly spent time in the Rift Valley with groups of students studying geology and physics.

My sister Joyce eventually married Imran Khan and the had three children, who seem to be typically Khan. They work hard to study geology, physical geology and chemistry and in their spare time wander the Rift together with their cousins.

The Rift Valley program was very successful and growing steadily under the gentle guidance of the Khan family. Eventually it would prove useful and liveable space where future generations could live, grow and prosper in safety.

My grandfather John was amazed that so much had been achieved during his brief lifetime: much more than he thought possible anyway.

Just one year and three days ago he passed away. His lovely wives, my grandmothers, woke that morning and found him sitting in his favourite armchair, gazing out over the solar window and beyond that, the purple black of the night sky studded by a thousand stars.

He had been dead for some time and was quite cold, sitting with his eyes wide open. He had evidently just drifted away.

Though upset, the sisters looked at each other, sighed and smiled.

"He's gone travelling again," said Sui. "What a beautiful way to end a wonderful life."

John Henry was just 84 years old.

Postscript

The Quiet One – William Henry Sums Up

I have tried, children, to plant a true a picture of the early days of our family as I can, but no doubt some of my writings will differ from your own memories. Please accept my apologies.

For some years now I have tried to keep a record of the people in our own circle, because to be frank I have lived a quiet life with few high points worth recording.

I had a good start with Mama Emma, but was inclined to curl up with a good book even in my younger days. Unlike my adventurous sister Joyce, my education was sound and eventually I did get through my university courses on Earth, though I didn't get a First.

Returning home to Mars, I took a teaching post in the Village school. The children were wonderful and listened to tales from Shakespeare, the Canterbury Tales and Beowulf avidly. I also was hooked on Mark Twain stories, which read well.

I was not popular then with the girls and the odd lass who bedded me soon wandered on. It was only when I was introduced to Mary Clarke, my new head mistress, that I became fully aware of lust.

A gentle woman, Mary agreed to marry and we settled quickly into an easy pattern. She did give me two daughters, Linda and Lucy, but died about a year later. Ma Emma, who had no children, took them back to live with her and David, so I joined them.

My life is comfortable, easy and well cared for, so now I have retired to write, at last.

~